A Dish Best Served Cold

Charlie Gardner

authorHOUSE®

AuthorHouse™ UK Ltd.
1663 Liberty Drive
Bloomington, IN 47403 USA
www.authorhouse.co.uk
Phone: 0800.197.4150

© 2014 Charlie Gardner. All rights reserved.

No part of this book may be reproduced, stored in a retrieval system, or transmitted by any means without the written permission of the author.

Published by AuthorHouse 09/30/2014

ISBN: 978-1-4918-8348-8 (sc)
ISBN: 978-1-4918-8349-5 (e)

Any people depicted in stock imagery provided by Thinkstock are models, and such images are being used for illustrative purposes only. Certain stock imagery © Thinkstock.

This book is printed on acid-free paper.

Because of the dynamic nature of the Internet, any web addresses or links contained in this book may have changed since publication and may no longer be valid. The views expressed in this work are solely those of the author and do not necessarily reflect the views of the publisher, and the publisher hereby disclaims any responsibility for them.

With thanks to my family and friends.

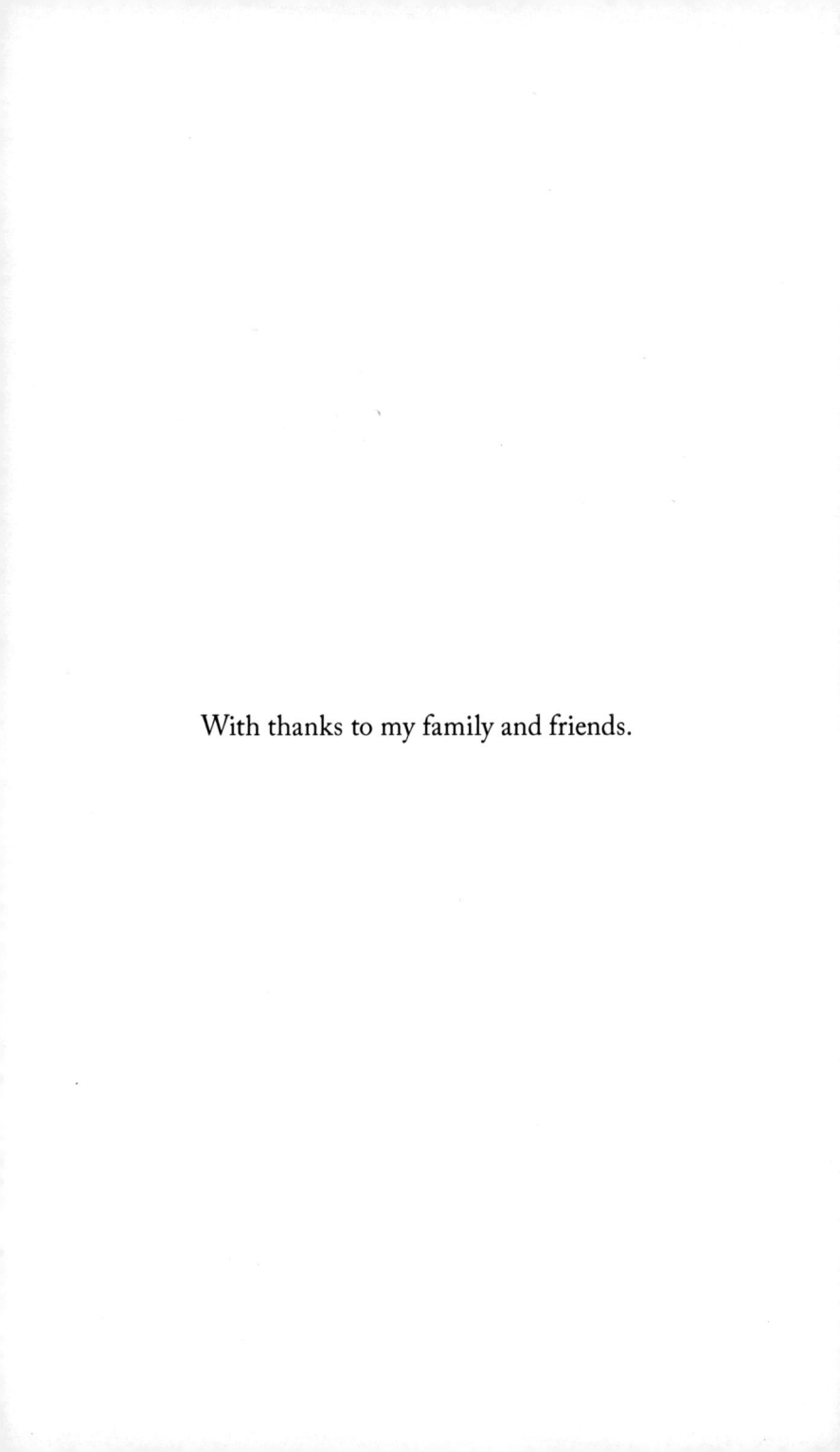

Chapter 1

The few weeks before.

Jake turned towards the woman laying next to him and studied her. The daylight was breaking and because Nina liked to sleep with the curtains open, enough light was seeping in to room to reveal the details of her face. She was asleep. Black. Not jet black but a dark brown, with a sheen all of its own. To Jake she was the most beautiful woman in the world and she was his wife. She had cared for him in hospital and they now shared a life together.

She stirred and her face broke in to a smile. "I wasn't asleep. I could feel you watching me. Umm, do you know what I want?" Her hand reached down under the quilt and made its way over his belly.

Jake rolled on to his back to enjoy her ministrations and as he did so, his eyes opened. For a moment his confused mind thought it was real then slowly his conscious made him realise he had been dreaming and the despair of reality hit him.

Tears entered his eyes and began to run down his face. This was not the first time he had suffered these dreams and been deceived. Jake put his face into the pillow and sobbed until once again he fell asleep.

Jake had now been a widower for nearly six months. That was over five months longer than he had been a husband. Nina had been his wife for only three weeks when he came home to find her dead. Shot by person or persons unknown. The police investigation had come to a full stop. From the very beginning, there had been little evidence to go on. It was as if the killer or killers had wiped the place clean. Drawers had been tipped out but there was nothing missing, not even cash and credit cards that were in the house. The police were baffled and still considered it was a burglary, disturbed early, with the culprits fleeing after being disrupted.

Jake was living in the house they had purchased shortly before marrying, and putting their mark on the property by generally tidying around and overseeing some painting, decorating and building work.

Having spent most of his life in the army, Jake had moved in with his mother, after being made surplus to requirements. This was the first house he had actually owned that he intended to live in. For three years, Nina and he had lived together in her flat in Wokingham.

Jake did not count the villa in Spain or a flat he owned as his home, as one was a holiday home, the other an investment and both were let to provide additional income.

What Jake now considered home, was situated in a back lane in a village called Riseley, about five miles south of Reading. Far too big for his and Nina's needs, they had talked of filling it with children. Possibly one or maybe two of their own together with one or two adopted, which was Nina's dream. It had five bedrooms, four bathrooms, and an enormous kitchen with a dining room, living room, utility room and a den cum office where Jake spent most of his days. There were spacious grounds and garaging for three vehicles.

A beautiful house, a beautiful village, and wonderful neighbours, but he felt dreadfully lonely. Yes, he had well-meaning friends and a loving brother and wife. His mother who had divorced his father years previously, now lived with Alf. He had been her next neighbour door when Jake first met him, and they telephoned or drove over every week. It was sat in his den playing on the computer or just staring in to space, as was often the case, that he found himself shedding a tear for Nina, realising what real loneliness is.

Friends and family could care for you and you could care for them. They would visit, invite you to social gatherings, which you really did not wish to attend, and telephone for a chat, or in the case of Dave Brewer his old army sergeant and nowadays business partner, to discuss the day-to-day running of their business. They all cared and yet it did not help dispel that feeling of being lonely. It was the need to care deeply for someone, a wife, partner, lover, and to have her care for you in return. For that hug, that was to reassure. Just a simple look, which entered your eyes, but registered in your heart. And all that had to come from someone that you would die for. For Jake it was Nina. And Nina was gone from his life. It also reminded him of Dzenita, another lover cruelly taken from him and murdered. Dzenita, whose picture was always in his wallet and his heart. When he had explained to Nina the significance of the photo they had both shed a tear.

Forget all the pills and potions that the doctors prescribe. Yes, they dull the brain and can help you sleep, but they do not provide a cure. Asleep you can forget, unless disturbed by nightmares and dreams. Often he would wake and for a moment or two believe that all was back to normal, only to become despondent when reality dawned. He had even tried drink, but a hangover is worse than the reality of the situation, because they are both there together.

The truth was, Jake wished to find the perpetrators of his wife's death and subject them to fear and then death and it was this wish that was going to get him out of this despair, and back to what was termed normality. He did not care how long it took, but it would happen. But not yet, he just needed to get to sleep.

Chapter 2

<u>Present day</u>

It was now ten months since Nina's death and I had been back at work in the plumbing and general house repairs business that I had set up nearly three years ago. It took a while to reintegrate myself in to the workplace and life in general, but with the help of my family and friends, I was getting there.

Nina still occupied my mind for most of the time and the frustration with the police for having scaled down the investigation was unrelenting.

Alf who had carried out the initial work of helping me set up the business, was still coming in three days a week. He had already retired once, but loved being able to prove to everyone that he was still well able to put in a days work when necessary. When I first arrived in Reading, he was my mother's next-door neighbour, and already retired from the water board. Now they were living together, but had told me they were too old to marry.

Dave, my old army sergeant was another of the original set up. We had been through an awful lot together and if I was honest, he had been the mainstay of the business during my absence. A true friend there had been no complaint regarding the extra workload. We had spent a lot of our life together in the forces, and when I tried to apologise, he just reminded me of the help I gave him when his first wife died of cancer.

He had now married again. His wife, Sue, the widow of an ex soldier had become known to us through her daughter Lisa. Lisa had been heavily in to drugs and that amongst other things had led to me being beaten up, kidnapped and hospitalised. After a spell in America at an Indian Reservation, she had managed to kick her habit, and was now working full time and training as an accountant.

It was my spell in hospital, which was responsible for my meeting Nina. A wonderful nurse who had returned me to full health.

Abe was still working alongside us. He had already rescued me once. Abe had lost his wife and child in a fire. An arson attack carried out by JJ, son of a taxicab company owner and drug dealer. Both of these villains were now serving time.

The group of us had even resumed our Friday night get together at The Pond House. For me it was better than returning to an empty house. I could still sense that feeling the others were treading on eggshells around me.

Ian and Manda were usually there and there was one addition to the group. Jason. Originally, he was Riley's heavy, but he had saved my skin after I was kidnapped and left to die, in an out of the way stable. He was now the proprietor of a car repair business. He had also done his best to protect Lisa during her drug taking days.

Although the sadness still pervaded my life, it was beginning to take on a semblance of normality.

Chapter 3

Returning from Pangbourne where I had been servicing a boiler, I dropped in on Ian. I preferred working on my own. That way if my emotions began to take over, I could quietly wait until I regained control. Ian's premises were next door and we often got together for a coffee

"Plenty of work Ian?" I asked.

"More than enough to keep me out of trouble and the debtors' court. Can't say that Manda is too happy about the hours I'm putting in. She doesn't understand that if we want a house and to start a family, then sacrifices have to be made. She's been moaning that we haven't had a holiday for over twelve months"

"House and family aye. That sounds great."

I do not know if he caught a slight change of tone in my voice, but he quickly replied, "Sorry that was a stupid thing to say. I know how much you and Nina wanted kids."

"Not at all. At least you say things and mention her name. That's what I like 'bout Manda. She doesn't skate around the subject, she talks to me and mentions Nina all the time. I didn't realise how well those two got on together. Everybody else would do anything to avoid it. Any way enough of that, you promised me a decent cup of coffee if I called in, and I've been here for five minutes now."

When I set up business next door to Ian, one of my first purchases was a Tassimo coffee machine. If freshly brewed coffee is not available I prefer tea. Ian was much the same and had also bought a machine.

"How about you?" asked Ian, "Do you feel better now that you're back at work? It must help to have something else to think about."

"Yes and no is the answer. Sometimes when there is a quiet moment it all starts to come back. What really gets me is that the police have virtually stopped any investigation. Unless some new evidence turns up, the case will remain on the back burner. If I ever found out who it was I would swing for them, and I'm not joking. I have so much hate for them, it frightens me."

"Don't fret over it; something is sure to turn up. Look how Alf spotted that Riley kid in a picture, when his mum and dad swore he was in Ireland. And you don't want to go taking the law in to your own hands. Give it time."

Ian slapped me on the shoulder and proceeded to make the coffees. "Sorry Jake but there ain't any biscuits; Alf called in yesterday and ate the lot."

We drank our coffee and talked over mundane matters and life in general. Ian's business was gold plating objects. Mainly this was for the electronics industry. He said how the price of gold was rising, and affecting his profits. Luckily, not all his contracts were fixed price and in some instances, he was able to pass the extra cost on.

"If you want a cheap holiday to keep Manda sweet, you can always use my place in Spain. Give me the nod and I'll check with the letting agent, and let you know what dates are free.

Leaving Ian's I walked back towards the road where Jason now ran the car repair business. Considering our first two or three meetings we now had a good relationship. When we met Jason was at least fifteen stone and on steroids. He had lost a stone and a half and kicked the drugs. His fitness regime was one evening a week at the gym and a three-mile jog every morning. Our gym evenings often coincided.

He spotted me as I entered his premises. "Morning captain, how can I help you?" He saluted and stepped over towards me. My title and the salute were his idea of fun and I think maybe a little respect.

"I bet you were an awful soldier, Jason. I'm bloody glad you weren't in our lot. Mind you, I was bloody glad to have you on my side a couple of years ago. You look busy; you've made a good job of this place."

"It's been hard work and a few sleepless nights, but I can cope with the ups and downs of it all now. I'll bet you didn't come here to see how my business was doing. What can I do for you?"

"Can we go and sit in your office? Look if you haven't got the time at the moment, call up at our place after you've closed, I'll be there."

Jason looked at me with a worried look on his face. "Are you alright Jake? If you want I'll stop now and we can have a chat."

"I'm okay. I need to ask you a few things, a favour really, but it will keep till later."

"If you're sure. I'll finish fitting these CV joints to this old wreck. Take about an hour and by then the bloke will be here to collect it. I'll come up and see you then, about five-ish."

The old wreck was a 1966 MGB rag top. It looked to be in excellent condition and I had noticed that over the last twelve months or so, more and older collectable cars, were being seen in Jason's yard.

Chapter 4

There was only Lisa in the unit when I walked in. She was glad to see me and was working on the credit control side of the business. She was a stickler for wanting clients to settle outstanding bills. A lot of our work came through the local authority, and they always owed us money. We discussed the individual cases for a while, and then at four o'clock I told her to have an early night.

I made myself a coffee and waited for Jason. I was not sure he could help me in the way I wanted, but this idea had been gnawing away at me for some time now. Although it may lead to nothing, I had to find out.

Jason strolled in just before five o'clock and I made both of us some coffee before we settled in to the armchairs in the office on the mezzanine floor.

"I'm intrigued Jake as to what you would want to ask me. My knowledge on just about anything is less than yours. You're an educated man and ex officer, so I can't see I'll be much help."

"All the education in the world is of no use to me at the moment. My army training may be useful, but one thing I do not have is street cred. You know people, you know how the dark side of life works, whether you can help me remains to be seen. I'm not going to ask you to get involved in anything you're not comfortable with, but I hope at the very least you can point me in the right direction."

"If I can help Jake I will. After Riley was put away most people shunned me, but you would always stand me a pint in the pub, and give me the time of day,where often I felt as welcome as a reggae band at a Ku Klux Klan party. Not only that, but you gave me business and recommended me to others, so that I am now able to make a decent living. To top it all, you managed what I never could, and that was to get Lisa off drugs and clean. That has meant more than anything. So ask away."

And I did. Jason was unsure whether he could help or even whether he still had a few shady friends who would be willing to talk to him, but over the next day or so, he would try.

*****

The Range Rover drove slowly up the drive that stretched across Prospect Park to a restaurant. The rear windows were blacked out, hiding the occupant.

The driver wound his window down about a third of its travel as the passenger in the rear lit up yet another cigarette.

"Rudy, do you think we can trust this Romanian gypsy? So far, he has never given a straight answer to a question. He boasts that he can deliver as much H as we require as well as anything else that we fancy. Nobody has ever heard of him, so how do we know it's not a set up?" The speaker was Joop Van Ess who was driving his boss, Rudolf Aken, known as Rudy. Since the death of Max and the incarceration of Igor, Rudy had tried to establish himself as a supplier to various other suppliers in the UK.

Success was only moderate due to the difficulty in getting coke, pills and crack in sufficient quantities.

"No Joop, you are right. We don't know him, but Sara says he was recommended to her by one of Max's old buddies. She has also visited Igor in jail and she says he checked with some of his old Slavic mates and they vouch for him. It is thought he is controlled by a Mexican cartel." Rudy lay back in his seat. In a short while, he would meet Erik Cuza, the Romanian gypsy.

Joop parked the Range Rover outside the restaurant and looked around. They were ten minutes early. He had only been driving Rudy for eight months. They had met whilst in prison together. Rudy's previous driver, Adri, had been arrested over two years ago on possession and dealing charges and was still inside on further charges. He vehemently denied the charges and was claiming the evidence had been planted. It had been. Joop was released earlier than Rudy but was at the prison gates ready to party when Rudy walked through them.

"Come on Joop, we will go on in and have a drink. We need a table by a window so we can see what comes up the drive to the car park. You get a table, I'll get the beers."

Although there was a sign requesting patrons to wait to be seated, Joop ignored it and made his way to a table he guessed would suit their purpose. The maitre de came over and was about to mention seating arrangements but with one look from Joop, walked away saying he would send a waiter to take their order. Rudy joined him with two beers and they sat in silence.

Rudy beckoned a waiter over. "Can I have an ashtray please?"

"Sorry sir but smoking is not allowed in premises serving the public. I will fetch your menus," the man replied before turning and walking away.

The waiter returned and was waved away after he had delivered the menus.

After twenty minutes, Rudy remarked "I'll give him five minutes and if he doesn't show we leave." Joop nodded. "I can't sit here any longer without a fag."

They were both so intent on watching the window that they failed to notice the man enter the restaurant and sit at their table.

"You Hollanders are so fixated on watching the smaller picture; you miss the world passing you by."

Both Rudy and Joop quickly turned towards the stranger who had joined them. Both started to say something but Joop yielded to his boss. "I take it you're Cuza and if you wish to do business with us, I suggest you keep your crass remarks to yourself."

"Having watched you two for the last half an hour, I'm not sure I would wish to do business with you. Anyway, it doesn't really matter what you say, the deal has already been done. I'm here to sort out delivery with you. Payment will be made from your Dutch bank." Cuza said this with a smile on his face.

"What do you mean the deal is done. I haven't agre….." Rudy's voice tailed off as Cuza interrupted.

"Sara and I have done the deal. No doubt, she is still meaning to tell you. She has asked me to set up delivery and means of contact with you. Look, you have your boss, I have mine, they never give us a complete picture, but we are the people that make it work for them. We take the shit, and we suffer the consequences when it all goes wrong. I don't need to be your best buddy, I just need to know I can trust you. You and your mate happy with that.

Rudy looked at Joop, who nodded. "Okay. We don't have to be confrontational about this, as you say we just need to rub along, and get the work done. Agreed?" The words may have been conciliatory but inside Rudy was seething. He did not like to start a business relationship where he did not have the upper hand.

"As you say, agreed!" Erik Cuza grinned, "And now to business."

Rudy and Erik discussed how the arrangements would work over a meal, with Joop interrupting occasionally, just like three city gents talking over finance matters in a London coffee house. The meeting was not easy for Rudy. As soon as he raised an issue or an objection, Cuza brushed it aside telling him that it was already agreed by Sara.

Chapter 5

Sara Meijer was thirty-eight years old. A blonde, like a lot of Dutch girls with the tall slim body of a model half her age. Not pretty or beautiful in the classical sense, but very attractive. She knew it, and she used it to get whatever she wanted.

Her eyes were pale grey, but mostly, with the aid of coloured contact lens, they were deep blue. Together with the expensive dental work, her teeth were shining white, in a mouth that may have been considered small, if it was not for lips that smiled at you and asked to be kissed. Outwardly the complete sensual package. On the inside a surgeon would never have found a heart. He may have found a cruel streak, but that would be all.

She had only ever loved three people in her life. Her mother, who had died when she was thirteen. Her brother Max who was murdered by East European gangsters, after his drug ring was exposed, and Inge. Inge had been her only true love outside of her family. They had met on a modelling assignment when she was twenty-two and were together for six years. They had lived together in a small villa in Southern Spain, until Inge was raped and brutally murdered while in Brazil on a modelling trip. Sara had vowed never to fall in love again.

When Max, who was eighteen months younger than her, was murdered she spent ten months in rehab before she was able to face the world again. She came out a different woman. Max, the one man she had loved and trusted, who had done his best as a boy to defend her against their brutal father. The father who had sexually assaulted and abused her since she was nine years old. He would take a leather strap or a cane to Max if he tried to intervene. If a strap or cane were not handy, then he would use his bare fists.

She had run away from home at sixteen and worked as a waitress in Breda, living with another girl in a two-roomed apartment. That was her first lesbian relationship, and although she did not feel love, she did feel safe.

Two years later she went back home. She told Max to pack a bag and to come live with her. When her father tried to stop Max from leaving, she grabbed a heavy iron poker from the fireplace and beat him about his head until he fell to the floor. Both her and Max then kicked him until he was unconscious. It was two days before his body was discovered.

The tinny sound of a pop song alerted Sara to her mobile. She fought the urge to leave it to go to voicemail, but recognised the displayed caller, and pressed the answer button. "Hi it's Sara, what do you want Rudy?"

"Sara, I've just met with Cuza. Why didn't you tell me you had already done a deal with him? I sat there like a plonker. I know you're the boss but if you don't trust me, just say so and I'll move on."

"Rudy! Rudy! Don't be so stupid, of course I trust you. Bloody hell man I as good as give you free rein over any decisions you make in my absence. I'm sorry and apologise for not letting you know of the arrangement I made with Erik. It completely slipped my mind. My fault but I've got so many other things on my mind, and so little time to deal with them. That aside, have you organised delivery?"

Sara listened to the details of how the deliveries would be made. She had no questions, for she knew that Rudy would have been meticulous in the planning. His freedom, if not his life depended on it.

Finishing the call Sara walked through to the bedroom to have a shower. She had not got out of bed until nearly midday and was still not dressed. She'd spent last night in a gay bar and had bought a young girl back home, where they had stayed in bed until the girl left at ten o'clock.

Getting undressed she secretly cursed herself for not telling Rudy about the deal she had done. Rudy was almost alone in the men she trusted. He was a friend of Max and had comforted her when she had returned to Holland for his funeral. They had even slept together, driven more by the need for solace than lust. It had never happened since and neither of them had ever mentioned it.

Chapter 6

A week had passed since Jake had spoken with Jason. Jake was in The Pond House enjoying a Friday night with Dave, Sue, Alf and his mum.

The banter was light and concerned the yo-yoing of the local football team, Reading FC, between the premier league and the championship. On seeing Jason enter, Jake rose and went to the bar.

"Hi Jason, I'll get this for you."

"You're alright Jake, I'm only having the one before I go home. I've been putting in a few extra hours trying to sort the paperwork out. The physical and technical side is easy, but the bloody bookkeeping leaves me cussing and swearing, plus an almighty headache. I suppose you want to know if I have made any progress with your problem."

"I actually got up to buy you a drink. I'm not expecting you to have anything for me yet. Come on I'll get a round in, and you join us over in the corner."

Jason started to object but Jake told him to join them, even if only for one drink. Jake got the round and Jason helped him carry them over.

The general discussion moved on and at ten thirty Lisa walked in and joined them. Jason was still there having got caught up in the conversation.

After Lisa had got a fruit juice and had sat down in a chair vacated by Jason, while he went to the toilet, Jake took the opportunity to ask, "Lisa, are you busy enough at work, or do you have the odd hour or so to spare each week?"

"Well in my less busy moments I manicure my nails, text or phone my friends, check what's happening on facebook. Then in the afternoon before all you lot get back to the yard, I pop in to Reading for a look around the shops. If I've got time before I go home, I sort out the invoices, books and do some filing."

Jake listened to her. "Okay, I know your day is fairly busy, and I have no complaints about your work. I know all about the manicures, use of the office computer and the shopping. I just wanted to know if you were able to make a couple of hours a week available for a new project."

She gave Jake a smile. "Course I can. Why?"

"Jason needs help with his books and I was wondering if you would be able to help? Not for nothing, but you would need to sort out with him what it would cost. Maybe free servicing for your car."

"He already does that. I'd do it for nothing."

Jason rejoined us pulling over a chair from another table. I should have known what Lisa's answer would be. Jason had been her protector from the worst of her episodes whilst hooked on drugs. As a bad lad, he had a good side.

Jake looked at Lisa. "Go on, tell him what you're willing to do for him."

Jason and Lisa talked quietly to one side for a moment then returned to join in the general gossip. Dave got up and said he would get the last round in, and I accompanied him to the bar.

"You okay Jake? I know you're back at work but I have experienced the loss of a wife and most of the time you wish you were dead yourself. Even though I'm with Sue, I still think of Maggie every day. She thinks of Chris every day and we both openly talk about them. We realise they're gone but they were a big part of our lives and although the hurt goes away, the memory is there forever. You never talk about Nina, unless someone else mentions her first. We all loved her and you'll find talking will help. I've known you too long and we have been through too much for me not to know that there is something going on in that head of yours. Don't do anything stupid and if there is anything I can do then let me know. All right! 'Nough said." Dave gave me a light tap to the stomach. "I mean it."

"Thanks Dave. I've never doubted I could rely on you. Things are tumbling around in my mind and when I can fathom it all out, I'll let you know. Life is pretty shit at the moment, and most days I don't even want to get out of bed. Mind you, there are many nights when I don't even get to bed. I come in to work to try and give my brain something else to think about."

Chapter 7

Jason crossed the road and entered the park. The man he was looking for was probably wrapped in an old army greatcoat, and huddled down in the corner, where two fences met, providing some shelter from the weather. It was late afternoon and the light was beginning to fail. He knew at this time of the day the man he was searching for would be in his usual place.

Striding across the damp grass towards the far corner of park, he could just make out what resembled a bundle of dumped clothes against the fence. Jason felt for the half bottle of whiskey in his coat pocket. There was a pack of four lagers in the carrier bag he clutched in the other hand.

Reaching the bundle of rags he stopped a good yard short. This gentleman was malodorous even upwind in the fresh air. He gave a sharp whistle. A grunted reply was received from under the coat telling the whistler where to go.

"Shiver, you old bugger, wake up."

The heap of rags mumbled. "Let me sleep. Clear off and leave me alone." The mans name was Shivers. Not his real name, because even he had forgotten what that was. He would sometimes say he thought it was Brian Stephens, but then again he could be wrong. Jason knew it was indeed Brian Stephens and that he had been in the forces.. No one knew when the name Shivers was given to him, but it referred to the involuntary shakes that wracked his body every five or so minutes. The spasms were not violent and at times so mild as to be barely discernable. He had been like this since his return from the Falklands, where he had been with the Para's.

"You'll sleep better with what I've got in this bag, which I'll let you have if you give me a few minutes of your time. Do you want them or should I go away."

Movement was more urgent now as first a hand, then a head appeared. The hand reached out. "Let's see what you got. Oh! It's you Jase, you should have said. You're alright, you are."

"Hang on a minute. I need to ask you a couple of questions. You'll get your beer, but not just yet. About a year ago a nurse was killed in a little village on the way towards Basingstoke. The police have hit a brick wall and although not closed, the case is barely ticking over. The bloke whose wife it was had a run in with Riley, when he controlled the supply of drugs about here. Now there have been a few snide remarks that he got what was due to him, but nothing concrete. The police still think it was a burglary gone wrong, but I need to know if there's any truth in the whispers."

"Bloody hell Jase, I'm no grass. I don't have anything to do with that rubbish, you know that. I know what you're on about. Bloke was ex forces wasn't he?"

"Shivers you'd sell your whole bloody family for a bottle of hard stuff. Yeah he was army, but he was one of the good guys and I'd like to help him. Any way this isn't grassing. I ain't no copper, and I won't be telling them anything you tell me. But you move around and you hear things. You know who is dealing and who is supplying. If they're the cause of this girl's death, as a revenge killing, then I bet you've heard something or know some one who does. Let me know who they are, and let me know who the big men are in this. Nobody will ever learn that you told me, I promise you that."

"The only ones I know about are the Turks and Omar. They struggled when Riley was nicked. They both have their own patch and avoid each other. I don't know who gets them the goods now, but I did here mention of a Dutchman. Now can I have my beer?"

Jason reached in to the carrier bag, produced a paper bag, and handed it to Shivers. "What the bloody hell is this? You said beer."

"It's a sausage roll and if you eat that first I'll give you beer and a drop of hard stuff."

Shivers ripped off the paper and crammed half the sausage roll in to his mouth. The amount of food in his mouth made it difficult for him to chew, but he persevered, swallowing some that was hardly masticated. The remaining half suffered the same fate. Holding out his hand he said, "I've eaten it, now let me have a drink."

"Here you are, you need to eat more." Jason handed the cans and bottle to Shivers who hastily opened the beer and took a deep slug.

"Look after yourself Shivers, and think about getting down the Sally Ann now the wet and cold weather is coming. Shivers if you hear any more on the street, then let me know. It won't go unrewarded."

Jason walked back the way he had come. It was about fifteen minutes to the units.

Walking straight past his own repair shop, he carried on to the top of the complex where Jake's business was located. He had seen Jake's Jeep parked outside so knew he was in.

The roller shutters were up so Jason entered and shouted for Jake. He appeared peering over from the mezzanine floor that served as an office. Jason began to climb the stairs when he noticed Lisa sat over in the corner, busy at a computer. He beckoned Jake with his hand and a nod of his head, retracing his way back down the steps.

"What's all the secrecy about Jason? Another one of your filthy jokes, too strong for Lisa's tender ears."

"No. I have a bit of information for you. Not much, but I will have a word with those concerned, and let you know what they say."

Jason explained what Shivers had told him. "It's not a lot but if it leads me to learning a little more, then it will be slowly, slowly, catchee monkee."

Chapter 8

Jake returned home to Riseley. The house that he and Nina had adored, no longer held the same appeal. He had considered putting it up for sale, but when the urge to sell got stronger, something inside of him held him back. This house had meant a lot to Nina and it was a tie he did not wish to sever. So much of her was in the fabric of the property.

To begin with he would climb in to their bed where he could, or at least imagined he could, smell her on the pillows and sheets. He had even put off laundering them, in case her fragrance should disappear. After a while, he began to dread getting in that large and lonely bed. He still could not sleep in the bed they had shared and slept in another room. Other than the kitchen, he lived in his den, where he would often fall asleep until the small hours.

He had always thought of himself as a gentle and forgiving human being. Yes, he had killed and had no qualms about it, but he now found he harboured dark thoughts. With regard to the death of Dzenita, he had always hoped that the International Criminal Tribunal in The Hague, for war crimes in the former Yugoslavia, would mete out justice to those responsible for her death.

With the investigation in to Nina's homicide almost closed, he knew he would explore every avenue in finding those responsible. He also knew he would kill them if he ever discovered her murderer. He hoped and prayed that Jason would find some way to put him on their track.

The telephone ringing disturbed Jake's thoughts. "Hi, its Jake can I help you?"

"Jacob, its Joseph. I'm calling to see how you are. It's been three or weeks since we last spoke." Joseph was Jake's younger brother.

"Sorry Joe, I know I promised to phone but talking on the telephone is not my best feature at the moment. I suppose I should be grateful that you all care, and its not that I don't appreciate the love and understanding you all show, but I feel so wound up and so inadequate."

"Why don't you come and live with Fiona and me for a while. The children would love to have you here, and you never know it may help you break out of this melancholy. It can't be fun being stuck in that large old house all on your own."

"Joe I know you mean well, but all I want is to get my hands around the throat of the bastard that killed Nina, and watch his eyes bulge as I squeeze the life out of him. Sick! Probably. Am I depressed? Certainly. Do I want medication? No. It most definitely would not be good for your children to see me now."

"Jacob you're in a bad way. Let me get one of my colleagues at the hospital to see you. It can't do any harm and it would put mother's mind at rest." Joseph was a Consultant at a local hospital having followed his father in to the medical profession. He was their father's blue-eyed boy whereas Jake had disappointed by joining the army as a private. Even his rising through the ranks to become an officer had not done a lot to appease his father.

"Joe! I'm depressed, not suicidal, and yes I would prefer to be here on my own, to grieve in my own way. I don't mean to be rude, but I'm going to ring off because I find it difficult to talk on the phone when it's not connected with work. I love you all and if I want anything at all, I will give you a call. Give my love to Fiona and the children." Jake put the receiver down, with a slightly guilty mind.

*****

Jason spent some time wondering whom he could ask to help him get some information from the Turks, Ishak Onder and Kaya Osman.

He knew it would be dangerous, and they were likely to be armed. In the end he had to admit defeat. He would have a word with Jake.

Chapter 9

The white van reversed in to the alley at the side of the Istanbul Grill which lay just off the corner of the Oxford Road. The driver got out and pressed lock on the key fob. Entering the empty shop, he beckoned to Kaya and said, "Shall I go through and unlock the back door?"

Kaya Osman was a cousin of Ishak Onder, the owner of the Istanbul Grill. The property was double entranced. To the left was a smart entrance to a restaurant, while to the right was a take away selling kebabs. Both were fronts for selling hard drugs.

"Ishak is in the back and will open up and check the delivery." Kaya grinned, showing a row of broken and dirty teeth. "Tell him I am busy serving."

The driver smiled, told Kaya he would tell Ishak that he was sitting on his fat backside, and walked through to the rear of the shop.

For the next ten minutes, he and Ishak unloaded the supplies in to a refrigerated store. Finished they both went through to a dirty and untidy room that doubled as an office and rest room.

Ishak sat in the only chair and told the driver to help himself to a beer out of a dilapidated refrigerator that stood in the corner.

The driver, who had never given his name, nodded and took a beer. "Rudy says the same terms as before and you know where to send the money. Said to tell you that the price of the uncut H will be going up for the next delivery, an extra five K."

"When I met Sara she told me they could hold the price for a year. You tell Rudy that if he wants an increase, then we will discuss it in seven months. Until then I will pay what we agreed." Ishak thumped the desk with his fist. "If he thinks I am going to line his pockets, then he needs to think again."

The driver shrugged his shoulders. "I only passed his message on. You need to argue the toss with him. No matter, I will tell him your reply." He chugged the remainder of his beer and got up to leave.

*****

A Dish Best Served Cold

Jake left the unit, not knowing where he was going, or why. It was Friday and the thought of another weekend made him shudder with fear. He knew he wanted to be somewhere else. The more he thought about it the more he wished he were not alive. No amount of pills and potions could rid him of his sorrow and gloom. He did his best to act normally around family and friends, but once he was alone the depression would set in. His conscious told him he needed help, but for some reason his sanity stopped him from seeking it. Numerous times at home the tears would well up and he would collapse in to his chair or on to his bed until the morning.

Ignoring his Jeep parked out front, he set off for the Oxford road. Turning towards Pangbourne for no apparent reason he strode aimlessly along. Up ahead he could see Tilehurst station. He crossed the road and headed towards the railway station. He stepped in to the ticket office and studied the timetable. The names were familiar with many a childhood trip. The idea of escaping Reading and finding solace away from his present hell was appealing. Checking he had remembered to pick up his wallet when he left the office he crossed the hall to the ticket desk where he purchased a ticket, and exited to the platform. Ten minutes he had boarded his escape vehicle. Finding a seat in a quiet carriage he settled down and after watching the countryside rush by fell asleep.

Chapter 10

"Rudy, this is a new patch for us and the last thing I need is Ishak Onder phoning me and complaining that after only a dozen or so deliveries, he's being told the price is another five thousand. We've put too much into this to piss customers off and lose them. There are plenty of others who will be only too pleased to supply Ishak and the like." Sara was holding herself in check. She was livid that Rudy had attempted to increase the price of supplies without speaking to her. She needed Rudy, he had helped her in many ways, but he would require watching. It had not been easy trying to re-establish her brothers business. She was also mad at herself for not telling Rudy of the deal she had with Ishak and Omar.

"Okay. Okay, I get it. Leave it alone for the moment, but we will need to take a bigger cut soon, or we will be out of pocket."

A Dish Best Served Cold

"We can increase the cost to some of them, I haven't agreed to hold the price for everybody, but Ishak and Omar, have a longer term arrangement. They are two of our biggest drops, and we cannot afford to lose them. I'll speak to you again tomorrow." Sara rang off, then thought that a call to Ishak would calm any troubled waters.

Ishak was arranging for the uncut heroin to be delivered to various family members, who would cut it and put it in wraps, ready for distribution. The crack and crystal meth would also be parcelled up. His mobile was ringing and he really did not want to interrupt what he was doing. He checked the caller ID and saw that it was Sara. He would have to answer this call.

"Sara. 'Alo. What can I do for you?"

"Hi Ishak. There's nothing I want except to apologise for Rudy's mistake in telling you there would be an increase in the price for H. He was unaware that you and I had a special understanding. As one of my valued customers I can confirm there is no increase. I won't keep you as I guess you're busy as usual."

"Never too busy for you Sara, but your intuition serves you well. I am sorting out deliveries, and you know how careful you have to be if you don't want the odd gram or two disappearing in transit. We will talk again soon. *Gule gule.*"

*****

Lisa was busy at her computer when Dave walked in to the office. "You seen Jake today? He was supposed to give a hand installing a wall-mounted boiler this morning and he didn't show. I've tried his mobile but it goes straight to answerphone."

"No he's not been in here today, but Alf called to say Pat was worried as he didn't turn up for lunch on Sunday, and he's not answering his home phone either. His Jeep has been outside all day. I thought he was with you."

"Bollocks! I'm worried as well now. He's been odd since returning to work, but that was to be expected. I think I'll take a drive over to Riseley and see if he's at home. He could of course have had a hospital appointment and forgotten to tell us." Lisa could see the concerned look on Dave's face.

Lisa was beginning to feel anxious herself. "Okay, you get off, and I will phone Abe, Manda and Ian to see if they've seen him. He's probably in a café having a Costa coffee." Tears were starting to form in her eyes. "He's a big bloke, an ex soldier, he can look after himself. He'll be alright."

Dave put a hand on her shoulder. "That's right. Jake's well able to look after himself. I'll get off." In reality, Dave was thinking of the number of soldiers he had seen crack up under the strain of a loss of a loved one or colleague. Big strong men.

Although the office was usually closed by five thirty, it was now an hour later and Alf, Dave and Lisa were sat there trying to decide what to do next. Dave had told them that Jake's house was locked up when he got there. Inside the front porch, he could see the weekend's papers, together with the post. He had a set of keys and let himself in, but he could tell no one had been there in the last couple of days. Nobody had seen or heard from him since Friday.

"Lisa, check the bank statement. See if he's drawn any money." Dave said hopefully.

After a few minutes Lisa smiled and said, "There has not been any cash withdrawals, but Friday somebody purchased a rail ticket, and the card number is Jake's."

At that moment there was a shout from downstairs in the workshop. "You lot are working late aren't you?" Jason's head came in to view as he climbed the stairs.

"Come on in Jase. We're trying to work out where Jake has disappeared to." Alf spoke. "You haven't seen him have you?"

"No. Sorry. What do you mean disappeared?"

Dave explained their predicament, and they then returned to rail ticket

Lisa searched in the Yellow Pages and then picked up her telephone and dialled a number. "Can you put me through to the Tilehurst ticket office please?" There was a pause then," in that case if I give you a transaction number can you tell me what the destination on that ticket was?" A further pause. "Look, that ticket was purchased with my company's card and I would just like to know the details of this transaction." Another pause, this time a little longer. "So you can't or won't help. How can I find this information?" Lisa listened for a while. "Thank you." She said putting the receiver down.

Dave looked at her. "Well?"

"Nothing. They can't give information like that without a court order."

Alf looked crestfallen. "What a load of bullshit. Since when has a ticket come under the Official Secrets Act."

"There may be a way." Jason had everybody's attention. "I use the railway quite a lot. There's a big black guy behind the desk and he is a friend of Abe. I think they're both in the same lodge or whatever they call it. You know the funny handshake brigade. I wonder if it's possible for Abe to ask a little favour."

"No harm in trying, I'll give Abe the heads up in the morning and see if he can help. There's not a lot more we can do tonight, but we'll get on to it again first thing in the morning. Now I need to get home to Sue before she reports me missing, and I'm sure you all need to be somewhere." Dave got out his chair, quickly followed by the others.

Chapter 11

Jake got off the train in Exeter. His ticket would have taken him on to Penzance if he had wished. He neither knew nor cared why he was there. He walked the streets for a while, until he noticed it was past nine o'clock. He did not wish to talk to anybody, even to ask the directions for the nearest hotel. After twenty minutes he found himself outside the St. Olaves Hotel on Mary Arches Street.

If he could have bothered to look, Jake would have seen a white painted, Georgian terraced property. He had no interest in the hotel or the cost of eighty pounds per night for a double room. Entering the hotel, he approached reception and asked for a double. Paying for three nights in advance in cash he mentioned he may wish to stay longer. When the receptionist asked about luggage he replied that he would fetch it from his car later.

He just wanted somewhere to lie down and be alone. He went up to the first floor and found his room. On entering, he took off his heavy jacket, threw it over a chair then lay on the bed and closed his eyes. Lying there, he knew sleep would not come easily.

*****

Rudy lit another cigarette. It still rankled that Sara had made private deals without letting him know. They were not exactly a partnership, and there would never be any romantic relationship, but he had done all that a man could do for her. Yes, she had the money and Max was her brother, but he was also a close friend of Max. After all was it not he that had put the idea of resurrecting Max's supply route, and of getting revenge on his killer, or at least the man instrumental in his death.

He and Sara had met a couple of times, at parties thrown by Max, but their friendship grew after attending Max's funeral. It was that night they had slept together.

Chapter 12

Tuesday morning, Abe, and Dave were down at the ticket office on Tilehurst Railway station.

"Luther, I wouldn't ask, but this man gave me a job and helped find Joy and Chloe's killer. It almost cost him his life. Don't you see I owe him big time? If it's not possible, we'll understand, but if you can help I beg you to find that information."

"Abe, this is highly irregular. Give me those details again and I will have a look. You don't have to beg me; we've been friends too long for that. Look, I'll not only get you the ticket info, but when I have the time of issue I'll sort out the CCTV footage for that time."

"Thanks Luther, I'll always be in your debt. We'll speak later."

"We will, and you won't be in my debt. This man deserves your help."

Dave and Abe walked back to the unit, where they found Alf up in the office with Lisa. They explained that Abe's friend, Luther, was going to telephone later when he had the information. Alf explained that he was there to help and it was better than being at home at this moment in time. Dave told them to get on with the day-to-day jobs, as Jake would still want a business when he returned.

It was late afternoon when Luther called Abe and gave him the details of the ticket, and told them that as there were only three people on the platform, he was able to pick Jake out. He was boarding the Penzance train.

"Well if it's all the same to the rest of you, I will be off to Penzance tomorrow to see if I can find any trace of him. I'll get off home and pack an overnight holdall, as I may be away for a few days." Alf rose from his chair and made his way to the stairs.

"Hang on a minute Alf. You don't know he's in Penzance. That train stops in Swindon, Taunton, Exeter, Bodmin, Truro and Penzance. He could be anywhere. I'll have a word with the police and see if they can help. Being an adult I doubt if there's much they can do." Dave continued. "Alf if I thought it was any use chasing around the West Country I'd be on my way now. Pat needs you at home with her right now."

"I know you're right Dave, but I feel so bloody helpless sat here waiting for something to happen."

A Dish Best Served Cold

*****

On the Tuesday Jake woke thinking it was morning, until he realised the room lights were on. He stared at the clock at the side of the bed. It flashed 3.11. He got off the bed and went through to the bathroom for a glass of water. Every day was the same. He grabbed a sandwich on his early morning walks, and then lay in the room all day. On the Monday he had to draw cash from an ATM. Feeling guilty about using the business card he drew the cash from his private account.

Jake knew that having slept for a few hours, he would not find it easy getting back to sleep. He would wait for it to get light then go out for a walk.

He dozed fitfully for a few hours then rising from the bed; he grabbed his jacket and left his room. There was no one in the lobby or reception area as Jake exited to the street.

A few early morning workers were making their way to their places of employment. Mostly they were to intent on their travels to notice Jake. After wandering aimlessly for thirty minutes he entered a newsagents and bought himself the Daily Mail, a box of aspirin, a round of cheese and pickle sandwiches and a two litre bottle of water. Even though he had paid scant attention to directions after leaving the hotel, it took only twenty minutes to find himself back in his room. The do not disturb sign was still hanging outside his door. The housemaids had knocked once but he told them all was okay and to leave the room.

He lay back on the bed. Alone at last, just what he wanted. Although that, was not what he wanted. He wanted Nina back with him. Reaching in his jacket pocket he found the sleeping tablets his doctor had prescribed. He shook two in to his hand, popped them in his mouth, and then reached for his bottle of water. He followed the sleepers with two aspirin, then laid back and closed his eyes.

Chapter 13

Jason pondered over what to do next. Gone were the days when he could lean on somebody for information. Today he was fitter and stronger than he had ever been, but in previous times he was recognised as part of Riley's mob, and in most parts that carried considerable weight. One thing he was certain of, Jake had asked him for help and he meant to deliver. He owed the guy. There was no doubt in Jason's mind that Jake would be back with them in a day or so.

He took a stroll up to Ian Nelson's electro plating business. Until Riley's demise, the two had a grudging respect for each other. It was only because they had both kept a close eye on Lisa whilst she had a drug problem that any respect between them existed at all. Ian and his girlfriend, Manda, had become good friends of Jake and Jason's part in his rescue had put their relationship on a better footing.

Jason stuck his head inside the unit. "Ian. You around, is it safe to come in?"

A voice from the rear replied. "I hear you Jase. Yeah come on in. What can I do to help you?"

Jason walked towards where the voice had come from. There were rows and rows of racking filled with boxes, various sized plastic containers and items Jason had never seen the like of before. The final rack against the wall was caged off and held carboys containing liquids labelled as dangerous in red. He spotted Ian knelt on the floor searching through a container of electrical items.

Ian looked up. "Hi Jase, what can I do for you?"

"Information, help, I'm not quite sure. If you're busy I'll come back later."

"No, I've got time. What is it you want to know? Tell you what, let's go and have a coffee and sit down,"

The two of them moved to a small area that had a couple of hardback chairs and a coffee machine. Ian busied himself making the drinks while Jason sat down and pondered what exactly to ask Ian.

Ian gave him a coffee and took the other chair and looked enquiringly at Jason.

Jason pursed his lips. "Ah well," he thought to himself. "In for a penny, in for a pound." He looked at Ian for a moment then spoke. "Do you still have anything to do with Omar, or Rupert as you call him?"

"As little as possible. I see him at family gatherings when he deigns to show his face. Few of us have any time for him. What is it you want to know?"

Jason explained what Jake had asked of him, but he had now reached the point where he needed help. The two possibilities were Ishak Onder or Omar. His presence no longer carried the fear that it used too, now Riley was gone, and he did not fancy getting in to strife with any of the parties involved.

Ian mulled this over in his mind then said, "I really want to help Jase, for Jake's sake, but I need time to think this over. I'll let you know tomorrow, if that's okay."

"That's fine, I know I'm asking a lot and I'll accept any decision you may make. In any case it may be irrelevant if they can't find where Jake's disappeared too. I mean with all that he must have seen as a soldier, and all that happened when he moved here. I cannot believe it has affected him the way it has."

"Dave told me that Nina was his first true love since a girl he met in Bosnia. She was murdered by some warlord and he took that hard. Twice in your life must be bloody hard to take."

"Trust me Ian, Bosnia was a shithole. Like all peacekeeping forces, you are fighting with one arm tied behind your back. The UN want to change their stance and let these people know that if a peacekeeping corps is sent in, then they will act with whatever force is necessary against any implied threat or act of aggression. No mucking about, you want trouble, then just raise a rifle and we'll strike with so much power, you'll wonder what hit you. Still, while we let politicians act as generals it will never happen."

Chapter 14

On Thursday, just before five in the evening, Dave was loading some fittings in to his van ready for the next day.

Lisa called out. "Dave I've got a Mister Rollins on the phone. He'd like a word with you."

Dave still had things to load and replied, "Ask him if it can wait ten minutes."

After a pause, Lisa's voice carried back down the stairs. "He says it's important."

"Okay, I'm on my way up>"

He reached the office and took the handset from Lisa, and then sat down. "Hi, it's Dave Brewer. How can I help you?"

"Good evening Mister Brewer, I am John Rollins. I'm a consultant at The Royal Devon and Exeter Hospital."

At this Dave sat bolt upright in the chair. "Have you got Jake there? Is he alright?"

"Yes and yes again Mister Brewer. He's resting at the moment and I've contacted you because he had two business cards in his wallet, both for the same company. One in his name and one in your name, which is why I've contacted you."

"You say you're a consultant at the hospital. Has Jake been injured or involved in an accident?"

"No Mister Brewer, and let me put your mind at rest and tell you how Mister Beck came to be here. He had booked in to a local hotel and because he rarely showed his face the manager became suspicious. Yesterday, although there was a Do Not Disturb sign on the door, Mister Brooks, that's the manager, decided to enter his room. Mr Beck was asleep, although Mister Brooks, in a panic, thought he was unconscious, and the sight of the bottle of sleeping tablets caused enough concern for him to call for an ambulance. He was admitted to the hospital, but I can assure you he had not overdosed. Yes, he is suffering a breakdown, but he only ever took two tablets to enable him to sleep and obtain respite from an unfortunate episode in his life. An episode he is finding great difficulty in coping with. I am a consultant psychiatrist, and have spoken with Mister Beck at length. He is neither a threat to himself nor any other person. I am happy to keep him in for another two nights, under mild sedation, as he is in need of rest, but I would like to discharge him on

Saturday morning. Is there anybody that could come and collect him?"

"I'll come myself. Tell me where and when. Thank you so much for calling. His whereabouts will be a great relief to his mother and many other friends."

The consultant gave Dave the name and address of the hospital and told him to call after ten o'clock on Saturday morning.

At a few minutes before eight o'clock on Saturday morning, Dave pulled in to Taunton Deane services on the M5. Time for a break and a coffee. With him were Alf and Jake's mum.

When Dave had given Pat the good news, that Jake had been found, you could see the years vanish from her. Having been a nurse in her younger years she was still concerned and telephoned the consultant the next day to find out for herself Jakes condition. That night in The Pond House, she insisted on going to Exeter with Dave.

With Jake's brother, Joseph's help, she arranged voluntary admittance to a private clinic, just outside Wallingford, where Joseph assured her that Jake would receive the best of care. All they had to do now was convince Jake that this would be the best course of action.

Jake was sitting in a chair at the side of his bed with his eyes closed, when Pat walked up, touched him on the shoulder then bent down and wrapped her arms around him. Pat had asked Dave and Alf to wait just outside the ward while she went in alone. Pat watched Jake rise to his feet as he caught sight of his mother and tears begin to form in his eyes.

Only five feet nine inches in her low heels to Jakes six feet one inch, she put an arm around him and then told him to let it out. Jake sobbed on his mothers shoulder uncontrollably for a good three or four minutes before mumbling sorry in her ear. He stood and taking a tissue from a box on the cabinet at the side of the bed, wiped his eyes.

Again Jake apologised. "Sorry mum, I didn't want all this to happen. I just needed to get away and try to forget everything."

"Don't regret it son, it's been for the best. Remember when you used to tell me about soldiers who lost comrades or suffered hellish wounds. You used too say they were shot to pieces. Well that's what has happened to you and you now need the help that they did. I'm taking you home and we are going to get you fixed up. Don't argue with me, but with your brothers help we have got you in to a private clinic to assist you back to full health. Dave and Alf are outside waiting to take you back."

Chapter 15

Ian had hesitated over deciding whether to help Jason. With Jake's return he was even more unsure if getting the information Jake wanted, was a wise move.

Jake had been in rehab for a month now, and he understood from Dave that he was likely to be there for at least a further month.

He had reluctantly decided to help Jason, provided they did not divulge any of their findings to Jake unless he asked for them. Ian also made it clear to Jason that until Jake was deemed back to normal, or as normal as anything could be that he would not even be told if he asked.

Biting the bullet, Ian decide to call on Rupert that evening.

His meeting with his cousin Rupert, or Omar, as he was known on the street, was fractious, to say the least. Omar was irritated that someone who avoided speaking to him at the best of times was now pressing him for information.

"You're asking me to give you help for a man that had me locked up. You have to be taking the piss don't you? Why should I help you?" A year or so back Riley had asked Omar to send a couple of boys round and to give Alf and Jake a beating and warn them to keep their noses out of his affairs.

Fortunately, Ian had seen them arrive and had thwarted their plans.

Ian threw his hands out to his side. "I am asking as a favour, and although we don't get on that well, we are still family. Whatever you tell me, I will never divulge my source. Look Rupert, I can't force you to tell me who is supplying you with the rubbish that is available on our streets but the word is that whoever it is was involved in the death of Jake's wife."

"Yeah we all hear the same thing, but nobody is putting their hands up for it. Just rumour, I expect."

"What if it's not just rumour? Tell me Rupert, who supplies you now? Are they involved? Who else could I talk to that may know something?"

"Hang on there man. I'm not giving you the name of my supplier. I've only just got my people back on track. I can't afford the cost of this going tits up again. If I don't keep on top, then someone else will move in."

Ian looked thoughtful then said, "if I ask the question and I am right, then don't answer, but if I am wrong just say no."

Omar did not look to happy with this, but reluctantly agreed after a little more persuasion from Ian.

Ian began. "Do you know who killed the nurse?"

"No."

"Was this new drug cartel involved?"

Omar shrugged his shoulders. "I honestly don't know."

"Okay. Let's put it this way. Is it possible that the talk on the street is true and this new gang carried out the killing?"

Omar stood his ground and said nothing.

Ian murmured his thanks, and placed a hand on Rupert's shoulder. "You're in a wicked business Rupert, but you are not completely bad yourself. I'm grateful." Ian turned and left.

Ian knew he would have to discuss with Jason what he had heard. It was nothing definite and they would need to find somebody who could add further information or even better confirm who the murderers were. He decided to call on Jason at the first opportunity.

The next morning Ian was outside Jason's premises waiting for him to arrive.

Chapter 16

The nurse entered his room with his dose of Fluoxetine. Jake had resisted the drugs to begin with but after a consultant had sat and discussed the benefit of an anti-depressant in his treatment he had grudgingly agreed. This together with daily counselling sessions, both in groups and on a one to one basis, was all his day consisted of. He had walked the corridors and visited every room that was open to patients and could now wander the building with his eyes closed.

There were no more than eighteen patients, if that was the right term for those receiving treatment. Most seemed to be withdrawn and kept themselves to themselves. There were two exceptions, both women. Both were heroin addicts. Jake met them about two weeks in to his treatment.

When Jake entered the day room, Gail was standing at a coffee making machine. "Would you like one?" She enquired, "I'm making one for Tina and me. I'm Gail by the way. I can easily make a third It's not bad as far as coffee goes. At least the lattes are drinkable." Gail was forty-two years old and successfully ran a marketing company with her husband.

Jake looked around the room and noticed a petite young woman sat over in the corner. "A coffee would be nice please. No sugar. By the way I'm Jake." He walked across to the table where Tina was sitting, thumbing a Vanity Fair magazine.

"Do you mind if I join you. You're the first people I've spoken to in the last two weeks that aren't nurses, doctors, or consultants."

Tina looked up. "No, I don't mind at all. You are the first man to talk to us in a long while. At least as a fellow in-mate, and not staff. I think Gail and me scare them off. Mind you there are only about three other male in-mates in here."

Gail came over with the coffees. "You'll have to excuse Tina, she refers to all except the staff as in-mates, as though we're in prison. Nice to have male company for a change though."

Jake smiled, then frowned as he realised that was the first time he had smiled involuntarily since his admission. "And it's very nice to have the presence of you ladies."

Tina studied Jake for a moment or two then spoke. "You look like a strong strapping individual, how did you wind up in here?"

Before Jake could answer, Gail butted in. "Tina! You know we're not allowed to question other patients as to why they are here. Jake may be embarrassed, or not want to talk about it."

"That's a stupid rule. They get us all in one room sat in a circle and ask us to talk about ourselves, for all and sundry to hear. I tell you more about myself than I disclose to everybody in those group-counselling sessions. You don't have to tell me Jake but I am a good listener and I don't repeat what I hear, and neither does Gail." She gave Jake a smile. "Let me tell you about me. If I see you nodding off then I'll stop."

Tina began her story. She was raised in Poole in Dorset by her mother. She never knew her father. Her mother died when she was thirteen and she was fostered by a couple in Maidenhead, who had known her mother. They were very loving and generous foster parents. She had tried tracing her father but with her mother now gone, it was extremely difficult, and she had all but given hope of ever finding him.

As a child she had loved singing, and whilst in Maidenhead had been in both the school choir and the church choir. At seventeen with her exam results behind her, she found a job as an underwriter with an insurance company. During this time she joined an amateur dramatic group and often took the lead part in any musicals they performed. At nineteen she was discovered by an agent, who put her

A Dish Best Served Cold

in contact with a record producer. She released three singles and one album. One of the singles made it in to the top fifty, at number forty-seven. She was dropped by the recording company, when expected sales of her third single were so poor and the agent found her cabaret and pub and club work. Whilst carrying out promotional for the recording company, the record producer had introduced her in to minor celebrity circles, where drugs were readily available. She began by snorting coke, but within eighteen months was injecting.

Over the past twelve years, she had been in rehab twice. Although prescribed Methadone, once back in the real world she soon sought the release and high found in injecting heroin. The singing work dried up and her agent tore up her contract. Thanks to the support of her adopted parents and the odd pub engagement, she had managed to exist. The reality was though, that she spent any money she had on drugs and not her welfare. It had got so bad, that after a court appearance for soliciting, her parents had a heart to heart with her and persuaded her to go in to rehab.

"But if you had already been in rehab and subsequently reverted to your old ways, do you think you will succeed this time?" Jake enquired. "I have a friend that went through a form of rehab, and she admits it was the hardest and most painful episode of her life, she ever experienced."

"If I'm honest I don't know if I will be strong enough when I leave here to refuse my previous way of life. None of us do. There are twelve inmates here, all on the same treatment. Usually in the UK if you go in to rehab you receive Methadone. It means you will be on Methadone for the rest of your life, unless they discover something better. The therapy here is a new way of dealing with the addiction. It was pioneered in Holland and Switzerland and this clinic has decided to give it a go."

Tina took a sip of her coffee then continued. "This new treatment is different because you are prescribed, over 12 months, Heroin up to a maximum of 1000 milligrams per day plus methadone up to a maximum of 150 milligrams per day compared with methadone alone of a maximum 150 milligrams per day. I only know all this 'cos I read it up when I was offered the chance to enter the programme. That was nearly three weeks ago and although it seemed to be okay to start with, I seem to struggle on the dosage."

"Me too." Gail intervened. "Everything was okay to begin with but over the last week or so, I feel just that little bit edgy before the next shot. I mean we've spoken to a few of the others and we all feel the same. But maybe that's how we're supposed to feel."

"I've never taken any drug that wasn't prescribed for me so I find it difficult to imagine what you call a high, or the buzz you get from these substances." Jake continued. "I have seen the harm they can cause and it frightens me that I should want to even try."

Gail reached across the table and put her hand on top of Jake's. "Don't ever lose that fear. Stay clear of the whole mess.. It ruins your life."

Jake sat back upright in his chair. Not because he needed to, but to withdraw his hand from under Gail's. It was not unpleasant, but the contact with another persons hand, especially a female, gave him feelings of guilt. He had steered clear of close contact with another since losing Nina. He noticed this had caused Gail to flinch.

"I'm sorry," she said. "I didn't mean to make you feel uncomfortable."

Jake gave her a smile and responded. "There's no need to apologise, the problem is mine. I lost my wife a short while ago and I do not seem able to cope with hugs, the reassuring squeeze of a hand etcetera, the whole tactile thing. At first I thought I could cope with it all, but then things went from bad to worse and I just cracked up completely. I wound up in a hospital down in the West Country, which is how I came to be here."

Both Gail and Tina gave him a big smile and Tina said, "Don't worry, everybody here has a problem."

Chapter 17

Jason arrived a little later than usual, having called at the auto factors for some spares and stock. He walked round to the back of his van to unload his supplies.

Ian joined him and gave a hand to empty the van. "Morning Jase, you ready for a coffee and a quick chat when we've got rid of this lot?"

"I'm more than ready. I think I can guess what it's about if you're waiting here for me at this time of the morning."

With the van relieved of its load they sat down to enjoy a coffee. Ian described his meeting with Rupert, and what he had learnt. "So you see Jase, we still have nothing concrete to work on. Do you know anybody else out there who may be able to provide an answer, or even a clue?"

Jason thought about it for a while, then spoke. "Yes and no, is the answer to that. Trouble is some of those I could ask may well let it get back to those responsible and bring a whole heap of shit down on me. I can do without that. I have got an idea that Shivers may know a bit more than what he told me. I'll try him again."

"Okay, but don't take any risks of it going pear shaped." Ian slurped the rest of his coffee then got up and made his way to his own unit.

Later that evening Jason took a stroll along the Oxford Road hoping to find Shivers in one of his many haunts. It took more than an hour, but he eventually found him in the old Brock Barracks site. Now mainly residential housing there were a few places that old soldiers like Shivers, could find to hide away. He was wrapped up in his greatcoat nursing a tin of cider.

"How you doing Shivers?"

"Hi Jason, got anything with you?"

"Maybe, but first I need an answer to a question. Do you know something you have not told me about the murder of that nurse. You remember the one I spoke to you about a week or so ago."

"Honestly I've told you everything I know."

"You sure of that Shivers?"

"Well there is one thing and it may not be of any use, but an old comrade I knows, sometime picks up bits of gossip."

"Who is he? I'll see if he can help."

"Sorry, but I can't give his name, the same as I wouldn't give your name to anyone asking. You understand that don't you. I'll ask him myself and let you know. Might take a few days till I find him though."

Jason reached inside his jacket and produced a cheese roll, which he handed to Shivers. "You know the deal. Eat the roll and I'll give you some grog."

"Bloody cheese, you know I don't like cheese, didn't they have any ham?"

"Don't be so picky you old bugger. I've seen you eat plenty of cheese sandwiches. Now I'm going to stand here 'til you finished it, and then I'll give you the bottle. Eat up, I haven't got all night. And another thing, get yourself down the Sally Ann even if only for a shower. The only way I could find you tonight was by sniffing the air as I went, 'til I caught your rank smell."

Shivers spoke through a mouthful of food. "You'd make a bloody good sergeant major you would. I bet you were a perfect little soldier."

"I was a crap soldier, but at least they taught me to stay clean and healthy. The best thing I got from the army was my trade. Now, stop talking and eat up."

Jason waited for Shivers to finish the roll, then handing him the half bottle of rum, said his goodbyes, and went on his way.

Chapter 18

At seven o'clock the charge nurse came in to Jake's room with a cup of tea and two tablets. Jake had been awake since just gone five and after lying in bed for twenty minutes feeling bored, had risen, and done a few stretches, sit-ups and press-ups to relieve the boredom.

As usual, half the tea was in the saucer, and Donald, the charge nurse did not hang around to see if Jake actually took the pills. It was the same in the evening, two sleeping pills dispensed, and in Jake's wash bag was over a dozen of them. The first couple of nights, Donald had actually watched them swallowed but had soon given up once he felt that Jake was actually taking them. Donald was an odd character. Jake reckoned he weighed about two hundred pounds but at five feet eight inches tall, he looked overweight by a lot more. His gait was a fast shuffle rather than a stride, and he appeared a strange sight pushing his dispensing trolley down the corridors. Donald, or

Don as he liked to be known was not what Jake would call a genial person, which he would have thought was a requirement in the nursing profession and at times even came over as sinister.

Jake finished his tea, then grabbed his robe and entered the shower. He enjoyed his time under the hot water; it gave him time to think. His emotions were still in turmoil. No matter what effect the pills had, or release the counselling sessions were supposed to provide, he still harboured an intense animosity for the person or persons responsible for Nina's death. He never mentioned this hatred either in the group or his one to one sessions.

Showered and dressed he decided to go to the day room for a coffee before his next meeting with the shrink. Jake felt a bit of a fraud, giving the psychiatrist the answers he thought were expected, but hoped that they satisfied him. Inwardly he smiled and thought if he told him just how murderous his thoughts were he would probably commit him to a spell in Broadmoor.

Entering the day room he noticed two or three other groups sat around, enjoying an early coffee. Gail noticed him and waved, beckoning him over. He waited for the machine to brew his cappuccino, and then took it over to join Gail, who was reading a paperback.

She put it on the table as Jake sat down. "Have a good night. Go any where interesting?" She quipped.

"Nothing special. Went to the pub for a couple of pints, then a whiskey to help me sleep." Jake responded with a wink.

"Well next time remember to invite me and Tina. The only fun we had was trying to catch Donald trying to catch a sneaky glimpse of us in our undies. I don't know what it is about him but he makes my skin crawl. Actually, I do know, he is a lecherous little sod that appears when he thinks your getting dressed or undressed. It's not only me and Tina; some of the other women here have said the same thing."

"Can't say I've had that problem with him, but I do find him odd."

"Odd isn't the word I'd use! Some of us here also reckon he's short changing us on our medication. Oh look here's Tina." Gail stood and indicated to Tina to get her another coffee. "If I drink much more of this I shan't be able to sleep at all tonight."

Tina joined them and the conversation returned to Donald and his creepy ways. She related to Jake of the day she told Gail, within earshot of Donald of how she was going to take a shower and then stretch out naked on top of the bed, because she always found it so relaxing. Without fail a half hour later, she and Gail watched sneakily from a slightly opened door from Gail's room, as Donald appeared outside her room. He had a quick look around to make sure no one else was about then rapped on the door and entered without waiting.

As he exited Tina's room, with disappointment written all over his face, the girls stepped out of Gail's room, laughing raucously. Donald's face was like thunder as his shuffling gait hurried him down the corridor. They both started giggling loudly on retelling the story. Jake laughed along with them.

Standing he looked at them both. "See you later girls; I have to get to my session with Professor Johnson for our little chat. Catch you soon."

Jake hoped he was being successful in letting the professor think that progress was being made. Even he believed that his mind was more settled if that was the word. That being so he still harboured dark thoughts, which he never mentioned to the shrink, and he knew these would not go away until he found who had murdered Nina.

Chapter 19

Jason was underneath an old MGB fitting a one-piece Abarth silencer. Gave the exhaust note a nice warble on tickover and a muted growl as the revs increased. It was also supposed to increase power output, but Jason had never seen anything to verify that. He was disturbed by a voice. "Are you Jason Barnes?"

Without coming out from under the car to see who it was Jason called back. "Who wants to know?"

"Constable West. Thames Valley Police."

Jason came out from under the four-post car lift and crossed to the office to see the constable leaning against the door. "What can I do for you? Not in any trouble am I?"

"No sir, but I would like to ask you a few questions. Just to see if you can help me with a few enquiries I'm making."

Expecting it to be the usual queries regarding cheap and shoddy foreign car parts, Jason was surprised when the officer asked if he knew a Brian Stephens. He confirmed that he did and then asked why.

"Mr Stephens was seriously assaulted last evening and is recovering in the hospital at the moment."

Before the officer could explain further, Jason intervened. "Is he alright? What happened? Have you got somebody for it?"

"Mr Stephens is as good as can be expected and will probably be discharged after a week or so. When he came round from the attack, the only words he has spoken was to let you know. I take it you can account for your whereabouts last night between ten o'clock and eleven thirty? Just to eliminate you from our enquiries of course."

Jason explained he was in the Pond House till half past ten and then went back to his lodgings. His landlady would be able to confirm that he was in by ten fifty as they had a cup of tea together and watched some television. He asked if it was the Royal Berkshire Hospital that Shivers was in, and when the officer nodded, told him he would visit that evening.

After the copper had gone, Jason wondered what could have happened. You often read of down and outs being set upon as they slept and even worse having flammable liquids poured over them and being set on fire by louts.

A Dish Best Served Cold

At the back of his mind was an even bigger worry. Had Shivers asked the wrong people, the wrong questions regarding Nina, and was being warned off.

Shivers head was wrapped in a bandage and he had a couple of dressings on his face. His eyes had never looked that good, but they were so dark, and deep within the swelling of the flesh around them that Jason could hardly recognise him. "Shivers you stupid old bugger, what have you been up to?" He sat down and lowered his head closer to Shivers.

The voice was croaky. "Bastards jumped me in the park. I've lost all me bits and pieces, including nearly half a bottle of rum."

"Do you know who they were?"

"Fucking Turks."

"The bastards from the Istanbul Grill?" Jason almost spat the words out.

"No, not them But I know they were Turks, I know accents and one or two of the words they spoke. I'd never seen 'em before"

It was enough information for Jason and he stayed with Shivers until visiting finished. He promised he would sort it out and would also visit again. Jason was seething with what he had learnt.

Getting back to his lodgings he made a few telephone calls.

The next morning at eleven he drove down to the Istanbul Grill. He wanted to be there before the lunchtime custom, Kaya was behind the counter when he entered. There was nobody else in the shop.

"Get Ishak out here."

Kaya could tell from Jason's demeanour that he was not to be argued with. He called through the door behind him for his cousin.

"Whaddya want now. Can you not even look after the counter on your own?" Ishak slammed the door shut behind him, at the same time noticing Jason stood there. He knew Jason from his dealings with Riley.

"Oh, it's you. What can I do for you? I haven't seen you for a long time, why now?"

Jason stared hard at Ishak. "A word of advice or if you like a warning, but first I want to know the names and where I can find the two Turks that beat up Shivers. Don't tell me you don't know 'cos I won't believe you."

"But I do not know these men or what you are talking about. Why would I?"

"Because Ishak, both you and I know that you make it your business to know all that happens around here, especially in your own community. So am I going to get an answer?"

"But I cannot tell what I do not know."

"Okay, to keep things simple, I say I believe you. Tomorrow I will call again and in the meantime, you find out who they are. As an incentive, I will explain what a shitstorm is. It happens when I contact a few serving paras and explain what has befallen their old comrade and how the Turks are responsible. This grill will look like Armageddon when they're finished. It will be King Richard all over again with the Crusaders taking on the Turks. This place will not even be suitable as a landfill site."

"You think you can threaten me. You are no one. Riley is gone. You can call tomorrow but my answer will be the same."

Jason shrugged his shoulders and left.

Chapter 20

At eleven o'clock, the next day Jason was back at the Istanbul Grill. Ishak was already in the takeaway.

With no courtesy greeting Jason looked at Ishak and said, "Do you have some names for me?"

"I have said yesterday Jason; I do not know the men you are after."

Jason turned to leave, but just before opening the door he turned and spoke. "His mates from the Paras won't be very happy, and they won't ask as nicely as me."

"Who are these Paras you speak of?"

"Don't know any of them, they're Shivers old Battalion. Don't worry you'll know them when they come."

Jason returned to his workshop. There was plenty to be done and he kept himself busy until his stomach told him it was time for a snack and coffee. Deciding he needed a word with Ian, he wandered up to his unit and gave him a shout. Ian made a couple of coffees and produced a tin of biscuits. In between mouthfuls of chocolate digestives, Jason informed Ian that he had been unable to get any further with his enquiries, and what subsequently had befallen Shivers.

"Is the old fellow alright? You say they took what little he had. When he's out we'll find out what he needs and give him a hand."

"Thanks Ian, I was going to do something for him anyway. It should help cheer him up. Poor old sod is scared they'll come back again."

"Christ Almighty Jase, this is getting too heavy. You need to put a stop to this before it's too late. I'm not worried about me but I would be about Manda."

Jason gritted his teeth then said, "I already have."

*****

Kaya was serving a young lady with a child when three blokes in combat trousers and T-shirts walked in and ordered three chicken kebabs with chips. The young girl left and as she did two other fellows moved from where they had been out of sight a few yards down the street, to stand each side of the door.

Kaya had his back to the counter when suddenly there was the sound of glass breaking and objects crashing to the floor. Kaya turned to see the glass cabinet on top of the counter in pieces and a stainless steel dish holding plastic knives and forks with some serviettes scattered across the floor. Kaya stared at the mess and then yelled for Ishak. The three men were now wearing balaclavas.

"Don't bother mate, your friend out back is having a little chat with a friend of ours. A little bit of information, he seemed reluctant to give up. Still to save his fingers maybe you can help us. You may even save his balls if he's being a little bit stubborn." Kaya looked at the man. He was tall, very tall, with big broad shoulders and muscular arms. His two friends were almost as big as him as well.

Kaya stuttered. "I..I..I don't know who y..y..you w..w..want." He spotted the long knife he used to carve Donner meat from the upright rotisserie and grabbed it, and then held it out toward the big guy. "Don't come any closer. I'll cut you." Not only the hand holding the blade, but his whole body was shaking.

"If you want to keep the hand holding that knife mate I would put it down now if you know what's good for you."

Kaya backed away and putting his free hand behind him for support, placed it on the hot bars of the grill. He cried out in pain and dropped the knife to free his hand to hold the burnt one.

All this time Kaya had been oblivious to the scream that was followed by a moaning noise coming from behind the door to the rear. He did not however miss the next howl that radiated through the building.

"Looks like your boss is being awkward. They'll start on his gonads next. Maybe if we start on yours, you may be a little more cooperative. How about we roast them on the grill." The big para drew a knife and made a move to the other side of the counter.

"No! No! Please I beg you I do not know these men you are after. It was the Dutchmen they wanted somebody to help them. Ishak told them to see a man with a market stall in Reading. I think he is called Ali."

"See how easy that was. Lets hope your not lying and I have too come back." He turned and shouted through the door "Leave him, we've got what we want."

There followed a blood curdling scream and a moment later a large black guy came through the door. "Wouldn't give us a name, even when I nicked his bollocks with my knife. Reckon he would have let me cut 'em right off." He laughed aloud. Joining the three in the shop, they removed there balaclavas, and walked out on to the street. The six of them strode quickly a couple of streets away where they climbed in to a people carrier and drove away. Driving towards Oxford, they were soon in the countryside, where they dumped the vehicle and set it on fire. Making their way through a small copse they reached two cars, then drove back towards the direction they had come from, turning off to the right at Tilehurst towards the M4. They needed to get to Tidworth where if ever asked, they would say and be seen as being on an exercise all that day.

Chapter 21

Jake now knew just about every inch of the clinic. Within reason, patients were free to wander anywhere. The consulting rooms, offices and patients room were out of bounds.

As part of his exercise regime Jake used the stairs to run up, that was until matron decided under health and safety, both his, and staff and patients, he would have to stop. Matron was a surprise. Jake imagined she would be a spinster in her late fifties and was astonished to meet a young woman in her early thirties. Either that or she looked a lot younger than she really was. Jake had never seen her in anything else other than a smart grey pinstripe trouser suit, and black shoes with a modest heel. In the afternoon of his first day, Matron had come to welcome him to The Aesculapius Clinic. Her name badge said Angela Bennet.

Unlike a large hospital, she was able to make a tour of the clinic every day. A bit of a stickler for cleanliness and tidiness. Some days she even accompanied Donald on his rounds.

Jake's outside runs were curtailed by bad weather. He did not mind running in the rain, but it was marking up the lawns, and matron had a word or two to say about that. Gail and Tina had joined him once or twice but could not keep up the pace.

"Have you noticed how everybody refer to this place as The Clinic. They never call it The Aesculapius do they?" Gail looked at Jake and Tina expecting an answer.

"Possibly because few people know how to pronounce the bloody name. I know I don't" Tina laughed.

"Oh Tina did you not learn the Roman gods and goddesses when you were at school?" Jake pulled her leg.

"No. I must have bunked off that day to look at the shops. I suppose that you went to private school and done all that Greek mythology crap?"

"I did actually. Go to private school and yes Greek history was on the curriculum. I should point out though that Aesculapius is Roman, not Greek."

"Well mister lah-di-dah public schoolboy, who is this Askypius? Bet you don't even know." Tina laughed.

Putting on an effected posh accent and smiling at Tina, Jake replied, "Aesculapius or Askypius as you call him, was the Roman god of medicine, which I think you will agree is congruous with the use of his moniker as a name for this clinic."

"Seems bloody silly to call the place by a name no one say let alone know what it stands for."

"I would hazard a guess that you would have named it The Dead Beats Centre."

Gail who had giggled through this exchange asked, "Did you learn all that at school. I can't remember bugger all about my history work, other than the teacher used to play pocket billiards throughout the lesson."

Gail and Jake laughed, while Tina looking blank asked, "What's pocket billiards?" Gail and Jake laughed even louder.

*****

Sara was fuming, "Why is it you cannot leave well enough alone or ask me what is to be done. Are you fucking insane. The Turks are blaming us for getting them caught up in this and you then try to start world war three by involving the British army, because make no mistake, that is who that little gang was. If it wasn't for the good news I've received this week I'd think twice about keeping you with me on this."

Rudy was furious; whom did she think she was talking to him like that. She would not have a business if it were not for him. He was the one who provided the contacts and ensured everything ran smoothly. She would never have known who her brothers contacts were and would never have met Erik Cuza. The last thing they wanted was someone poking their nose in their business and getting the police interested. It was hard enough setting everything up, just for some loose tongue to bring it all crashing down. Sara may be rich enough to survive but he needed the money.

Losing his cool, Rudy shouted down the telephone. "I don't care what you say Sara, but somebody had to let these people know that they need to button their lip. That is how Max kept control of any situation. Give in once and you'll lose everything. You need me Sara, I know this business inside out. There are some very nasty people around who would think nothing of wasting you and taking control. What is this good news you have received."

"I don't care what you say Rudy, in future you ask me before making those kinds of decisions. Those same nasty people will also be quite happy to work with me. Oh yes, the good news, Beck is in an institution having suffered a breakdown." Sara slammed the receiver down.

"Can you believe that Joop. The silly bitch has just had a go at me for showing these people that we don't stand for any nonsense." Rudy stubbed out his cigarette and immediately lit another one.

"You want to cut down on those bloody things. You ever thought what they're doing to your insides. Your lungs must be black." Joop looked hard at Rudy. "You also need to pay a bit more attention to what Sara tells you. Having that old vagrant beaten up was not your smartest move. The Turks are pissed off that you have embroiled them in this and Ishak is telling Sara, he wants you to pay for the damage to his takeaway."

Rudy cut in. "He can piss off. He's already getting his supplies cheap. If he wants to push it, I'll soon show him what real damage to his shithole really is."

Chapter 22

Over the past three days, Jake had watched Donald return to his little office that served as the pharmacy. Normally locked, he would leave the door open when he was in there working. Built in as part of the corridor, the room was about three metres long by two metres wide. The front was a low wall for its entire length topped off with glass up to the ceiling. There was a sliding panel in the glass, for dispensing the pills and potions, although this was now secured, and no longer used. The door was at the end of the construction where the hallway made a left turn. The door was built in to this partition.

Working on the counter, mixing and dispensing his potions, Donald looked out across the hallway and would not be aware of Jake sat along the hall on a bench, studying his every move through the open door. If spotted Jake intended to take his shoe off and appear to be tipping out some object that had been annoying him.

The odd thing was the package Donald made up from items in the dispensary, which he then handed back to the driver from the pharmaceutical company. He decided this was just returned drugs that were not required.

Realising that Donald had almost completed his chores, Jake made his way to the day room where he hoped to find Gail and Tina.

Neither Gail nor Tina was there so he made a coffee and reclining in an armchair, he closed his eyes to think things through.

It was twenty minutes later that he woke to find Gail and Tina sat opposite, laughing at him. Still laughing Tina said, "Hi sleepyhead, had a good rest?"

It took a few moments for Jake to come to his senses. "I must have needed that. I haven't enjoyed forty winks like that for a long time." He closed his eyes and tipped his head back.

"Well your good company I must say. We make the effort to come and see you and all you can do is sleep." Tina picked up the coffee that Jake had made earlier. "Would you like me to get you a fresh cup, this one has gone cold."

"Thanks Tina, I'd love a cup, and you'd better put two shots in it. I need something to wake me up."

As Tina departed, Jake looked across at Gail. "When Tina gets back there's something I'd like to discuss with you two."

*****

"That's all I fucking need. A month's supply seized by Customs. The driver is in the slammer and the brief says that the border guards said they were looking for illegal people trafficking. Seems too bloody convenient to me." Rudy was pacing up and down the room. "Too much of a coincidence I'm thinking. First Adri on some trumped up charge, and now this. Makes me think there's a leak somewhere. I tell you Joop, I wouldn't put it past that bastard Cuza to be involved, so that he can pick up the pieces." Ceasing to stride, he stopped and lit a cigarette.

"Can't see it myself boss but I suppose it is possible. What does he gain though? At the moment, he sells to us and we have the risk of distributing it around our people. Unless of course he has somebody else lined up as a partner to take control of our end."

Muttering away to himself, Rudy continued to march backwards and forwards until finally taking a seat, and punching in a number on his speed dial. After a few moments, he threw the mobile down. "Even fucking Sara can't be bothered to answer her phone."

"You need to calm down Rudy. You'll give yourself a heart attack if those damn cancer sticks don't get you first. She's probably somewhere that it's not convenient to answer your call, or she's still in bed. It's still only nine thirty in the morning and we both know that if she's been out partying, she's unlikely to get up before midday."

Sara had indeed been partying and was curled up in bed with Viona, a young blonde girl of twenty-two that she had met in a bar a few weeks previously. The name Viona suited her as it meant fair and white. If she had bothered to look were nine missed calls on her mobile, mostly from her legal advisor regarding the apprehension of the driver, now in police custody.

As it was, a call of nature forced Sara to get up at five minutes to eleven o'clock. As she clambered back in to bed, she noticed her mobile flashing away on the bedside table. Initially she thought to ignore it but being half awake decided to look and see who had tried to get hold of her. Picking up the phone, she went through to the kitchen and put the kettle on to boil. Viona remained fast asleep in bed.

Returning the call to her legal advisor, Niels de Groot, she was surprised to learn the news of the driver's arrest. The driver was sticking to the story that he knew nothing of the drugs and he was being used surreptitiously to ferry them from Holland to the UK. He had told de Groot that he would stick to his story and hope for the best, provided his family were taken care of. Sara told de Groot to arrange an immediate payment to the mans wife and let her know that monthly payments would be made.

Chapter 23

The blue telephone in Katrijn Spronk's office rang just as she was about to leave for lunch. She returned to her desk and picked up the receiver. The blue telephone number was only known by a few agents. and all calls were scrambled.

"Hi, it's Katrijn, do you have anything to report?"

The voice the other end said no new report, and that they were just checking in. They would report again in the next forty-eight hours as usual.

"Okay, that's fine. Just to let you know that your last report bore fruit and we have the driver in custody, and have seized drugs worth nearly a quarter of a million Euros."

Katrijn placed the receiver back on its cradle. At thirty-three she was one of the departments youngest Inspectors. She had joined the Korps Landelijke Politiediensten, the

National Police Services Agency, at the age of twenty-two after studying criminology at university. She was attached to the Dienst Nationale Recherche, the National Crime Squad, dealing with cross border crime and dealing with her counterparts in other countries. Within the DNR she was tasked with tackling the crimes of drug smuggling and people trafficking. A lot of this work involved undercover agents and intelligence gathering.

*****

Following his talk with Tina and Gail and further surveillance, Jake believed he had fathomed out what Donald was up to. Problem was he had no proof and did not know how to get it.

It took two days deliberation before Jake resolved his dilemma by telephoning Thames Valley Police HQ.

"Good morning, are you able to put me through to D I Bill Talbot? The last time I spoke with him he was stationed at Castle Street Reading."

"Do you have an extension number?"

"Sorry but I haven't spoken with him for over three years."

"Hold the line; I'll try to find him for you."

Jake was beginning to think he had been cut off, when the operator spoke. "Sorry but D I Talbot retired eighteen months ago. I can put you through to C I D in Reading if you wish."

Not sure what to do, Jake replied, "No that's alright, I'll leave It," and pressed the call finished button.

He lay back on his bed and pondered what to do next. He knew a solution but was unsure if the person involved could help. He tried to think of an alternative. Other than walking in to a police station and telling them of his suspicions, he knew that his earlier thought was the best one. He began a name search on his mobile.

Chapter 24

"About time to Sara. Do you know what's been happening?"

"Calm down Rudy, of course I know what has happened. Niels has apprised me of the situation and all is okay. Jan the van driver will keep shtum as long as we provide for his wife and children. I don't know how this happened and Jan seems too think that the police knew in advance."

Rudy interjected. "Yeah, by that crooked piece of shit, Cuza. He wants our business, and is setting about getting it."

"I would not like too think that Cuza is playing silly buggers but he would have a lot to gain if we were out of the picture."

"I never did like the bloke and I wouldn't trust him farther than I could throw him. Problem is that he always knows when shipments are to be made. Still if you and I keep the details to ourselves then it can only be one of three people, and you and I have nothing to gain."

The two of them spoke a while longer and Sara gave Rudy details of a shipment that was being arranged to ensure that their contacts did not start looking for supplies elsewhere.

*****

Having found the number he was after, Jake was dismayed, but not surprised that it was no longer a serviceable user. Having got this far Jake appreciated that he could not leave it be. His own conscience would not allow it to rest. He dialled the number for Fleet police station and was put through to a central number.

Once again he was thwarted but the operator took his number and would pass it on. Jake was not confident that his call would be returned, but surprise, surprise, only an hour or so later there she was returning his call.

"Jake Beck, there's a blast from the past. How are you, I haven't spoken to you for what must be three years. What can I do for you?"

"Sergeant Gill, it's good of you to return my call. I suppose it has been three years. I hope you're well and enjoying life. Thanks for your thoughts regarding Nina and for the flowers and kind remarks at the funeral. I'll not beat about the bush, but I need your help and advice."

"Firstly let me say I was sorry to hear about your wife. She seemed a fun lady the once or twice we met. I have asked Joe Hopkins, the DI in charge of the case for updates, but it does seem to be in a rut at the moment. Still I know he is doing what he can to get justice for Nina. Now, how can I help you? And I should say it's Inspector Gill now, but you can call me Jen, we go back too far to be so formal, unless of course I have to arrest you."

"Inspector eh! Well it must have been richly deserved, I doubt that the powers that be give away rank and salary increases for nothing."

"Thank you."

"I tried to get hold of Bill Talbot but I'm told he's now retired." Jake went on to explain where he required help. Inspector Gills was unable to help but said she would get a colleague that she had met at the Police Training College at Bramshill to call him. They reminisced for a while and Jen again said how sorry she was to have heard of Nina's death before ringing off.

The next day Inspector June Welford of Thames Valley Police called and spoke with Jake. He explained what he had seen and Inspector Welford asked that he give her a while to mull over and consider what he had told her. Jake thanked her and remarked that he hoped he was not wasting her time.

Reflecting on the action he had taken Jake felt he could do no more and it was now up to the authorities to act if they so wished.

A Dish Best Served Cold

*****

"Joop you lazy bastard, we're going for a ride. I need to check a few things out."

"Give me five minutes to eat this pizza and then I'll be ready. Where are we going?" Joop pushed another piece of the Quattro Formagio in his mouth.

"You've got ten minutes while I have a fag and a crap. I need to look at some derelict properties in a lane off the Oxford Road in Reading. Thinking of going in to the property development business." Rudy picked up his cigarettes and lighter, and went through to the toilet.

Sipping on a glass of cola, Joop was startled when Rudy's mobile burst in to some awful tune and began to vibrate. Joop looked at the screen but there was no caller name and just two words. Two days.

He was just finishing the last of his supper when Rudy returned. "You ready now?"

"I'm okay, let's go." Joop mumbled through a mouthful of food.

They both climbed in to the Range Rover and Joop pulled out on to the road. "Where we going Rudy?"

"Take me to the Istanbul Grill. I fancy a kebab." Rudy leaned back and lit a cigarette. They drove in silence and did not even talk as they parked and walked to the restaurant. As they entered Rudy made for a table where a youth of about twenty and his girlfriend were about to be seated.

Pulling the lad to one side Rudy sat down and indicated for Joop to sit in the chair opposite.

"Hey mate this is my table, you can't just push in."

Rudy looked up at him. "There are plenty of tables over there, why don't you just take the young lady over there and study the menu."

The young man did not move and stared at Rudy. "You need to be taught some manners. In this country we queue and wait to be seated, not just push in." He stepped forward to crowd Rudy.

Rudy stood and gave him a hard stare. "Look, I'm going to sit here and you are going to sit over there. Don't threaten me or you will be unable to chew your meal and will be shitting teeth for a week."

The boy's girlfriend pulled on his arm. "Chris, leave it we don't want any trouble." She tugged harder on his arm to move him on his way, then turned and looked at Rudy. "Bloody foreigners."

Other diners had either looked fixedly at their food or gaped openly at what had taken place. The only waiter present had backed off to the serving door.

Joop sat the opposite side of the table. "Did you have to do that. He was causing no harm and it was his table." He beckoned a waiter over. "Ask that young couple to choose a bottle of wine and put it on my bill please. Tell them it's with apologies."

"You soft bastard. I was hoping he would take a swing at me."

A waiter appeared and gave them each a menu. "Good evening gentlemen, can I get you a drink before you order?"

Rudy looked at him. "Yes you can. You can tell Ishak to get his arse out here now."

"Pardon sir." The waiter looked puzzled.

"I said tell Ishak to get his arse out here now. Do you understand, or should I repeat it again."

For a moment or two Joop leaned back in his chair and shook his head from side to side. "What the hell has gotten in to you? You've been like a bear with a sore head ever since you spoke to Sara."

Before Rudy could answer Ishak appeared. *"Buyurun.* What is your problem? Why do you come here disturbing my customers and humiliating me in front of my staff. If there is a problem come out the back to my office and tell me what is wrong, but do not come in to my restaurant and embarrass me or we shall fall out."

"Ishak you greasy little shit, don't you dare threaten me or this place will burn down with you in it. Now I need the answers to some questions and if I think you are lying then there will be a big falling out."

"Ask your questions, I have no need to lie to you."

"Have you been speaking with Cuza?"

"Who? I don't know any one called Cuza. Who is this person that I should want to talk with him?"

"Doesn't matter. Who else is supplying you with drugs?"

"Nobody, what is it with all these questions. You are my only supplier, why would I need to go to somebody else."

Rudy pondered over Ishak's replies. He had no reason to lie and Rudy had no reason to disbelieve him. However things were happening for which he had no answer. "Let me know if you're approached by another supplier. Meanwhile Ask your staff to get me a chicken kebab and salad and the same for Joop. We'll also have a couple of beers."

Ishak rose from the table. "I will arrange for your order and Rudy, I deal with you and Sara. I like Sara she has always been straight with me. You are okay but not when you're in this mood. I will let you know if I am offered a better deal. Have your meal on the house, but please do not come here upsetting my customers."

After Ishak had left Joop asked, "What the hell is that all about. Is somebody trying to muscle in on our patch?"

In hushed tones Rudy told Joop all about the conversation he had with Sara earlier, and his worries that the arrest of the driver and loss of supplies was down to somebody selling them out.

Joop puffed his cheeks and exhaled loudly. "What makes you think Ishak is involved? We've never had reason to doubt him."

"Just one little doubt eradicated. I believe Ishak was telling the truth. Something isn't right though. I don't know what it is and I don't like not knowing."

There kebabs arrived and Rudy picked at his chicken muttering away to himself throughout the meal.

Chapter 25

Ian was sat in the café enjoying his coffee when he saw Alf walking past the window. Quickly jumping up he rushed to the door. "Alf," he called out. "Alf, come and have a coffee."

Alf turned and walked the few paces back to the café. "Love to Ian, but I need to get to the unit and let Lisa get off to the dentist. Come on up to the office later and we'll have one there."

Ian agreed to call later and went back in to the café to finish his drink. He decided he would see Jason on the way back and ask him to accompany him when he went to see Alf.

It was gone eleven thirty when Jason gave Ian a shout, and they both went next door to see Alf.

"Come mob handed have you?" Alf grinned at the two of them.

Ian had a serious look on his face. "Not really Alf but we have something we need to discuss."

"Well in that case, I had better get a brew on, and then we can sit down and I can hear what you have to say." Alf busied himself with the kettle, teapot and cups.

Seated with a mug of tea each, Ian explained what Jake had asked Jason to find out and how it had led to shiver's beating. Things had changed when Jake went AWOL and then was admitted to The Aesculapius Clinic.

Alf looked amazed. "I don't believe what I'm hearing. What makes you or Jake think that you can solve this where the police can't. No wonder the silly sod is so mixed up he doesn't know if he's on his head or his arse."

"Look Alf all this happened because at the time it was thought Jake was through the worst of it. In a few weeks, he will be out and you know what he's like, he'll be asking for answers. Some of it he already knows, so Jason can't just act dumb. You've been to see him once while he's in the clinic whereas we have no idea how he's progressing."

"Oddly enough he seems better now than he has ever been but that could be the drugs. He's made friends with a couple of women in there and you'd think he was on holiday. His brother Joseph keeps his mum and me up to date as they're not to keen on visitors as you know. I would leave it till he comes home, If he asks, then tell him because if he found out later that you'd kept something from him, you know Jake, he'd go spare."

*****

Sara slapped Viona across her buttocks. "Vee go and make us both some coffee, I'm absolutely parched. I've never known a girl with as much stamina as me. I need a shower after all that."

Viona climbed out of the bed and grabbed a robe to cover herself. "I will make coffee but first I will also have a shower. You can join me if you like or lay there and wait."

Sara showed her intention by rolling over and closing her eyes.

Twenty minutes later Viona called from the kitchen to say coffee was ready and that she had warmed some croissants. Sara entered the kitchen in a robe, but not yet showered sat down, took a gulp of coffee, then heaped some jam on a plate, split and spread a croissant, which she quickly devoured.

"I have to make a few calls, but afterwards we can go shopping. We'll go down to Kalverstraat. I've seen some lovely clothes in Maison de Bonneterie. Right, I'm going to have my shower and get dressed."

After showering, Sara called Rudy. "I've been thinking over what you said and you may be right about somebody trying to muscle in on our business. Other than you, and me nobody knows of the shipments except Cuza and whoever is looking after his end of the trade. I have spoken with Cuza and he is adamant that the leak is not his end. That only leaves us two and Joop. How well do you know him?"

"I met him in prison eight years ago. I was in for assault and grievous bodily harm and he was in for robbery with violence. We shared a cell and got to know each quite well. He was a hard bastard inside and between the two of us managed to keep the loonies of our backs. He got out four months before me, and on my release, met me outside the prison with a stretched limo stacked with booze and five young ladies. We booked in to a hotel and didn't hit the streets for nearly a whole week. I would trust him with my life, hell I would even trust him with my wife if I had one."

"Well I can't see who else it can be. Nobody else knows about the shipment dates or the routes that we use. Keep your ear to the ground Rudy and let me know if you discover anything. Speak soon."

Chapter 26

Jake, Tina and Gail were sitting drinking coffee when a nurse came in and asked if Jake could go to the matron's office.

"Wonder what rule I've broken now. Matron asked me if I had a problem with authority a few days ago. Told me I was a bad influence on the other patients here. Suppose I had better show willing and attend the summons."

Jake rose from his chair and made his way to the office. He knocked and entered to find the matron and another woman. Both stopped talking as he entered.

"Ah, hello Jake, this is Inspector Welford of Thames Valley Police. I believe the two of you have already spoken." As matron introduced the Inspector, she also indicated for him to take a seat. Jake shook hands with June Welford, mouthed a silent hello and sat down.

Matron looked at Jake. "As I gather you already have some knowledge of why the Inspector should be here, I will let her tell you what has happened."

The Inspector turned her chair towards Jake's, and related the events of the past day. "Normally, I will admit, that we would be very careful before acting on information from the public, let alone somebody undergoing treatment in a clinic, but Jenny Gills convinced me that you were not a time waster and if you had something to pass on, it would be worthwhile looking in to."

At this point matron interrupted to ask if they would like tea or coffee. Both said yes to coffee and matron buzzed through on her intercom to ask her assistant to bring a fresh pot to her office.

The Inspector continued. "Earlier today, following his delivery of drugs to the clinic, we stopped and searched the van and discovered a package of high grade Heroin and various other class A and Class B drugs. The van driver, a certain Barry Jones, was arrested and will be charged later. He has already dropped your friend Donald, deep in the mire. He was arrested at home about half an hour ago. We arrested him at home to avoid any unnecessary bad publicity for the clinic. He hasn't admitted to anything yet, but the evidence is overwhelming. What I would like to know is what put you on to this."

Jake face broke in to a smile. "Since I've been in here I have made friends with two women on a new type of addiction rehabilitation. They mentioned that sometimes the effect of their drug relief was short-lived and not as powerful. I asked them to let me know which days this occurred.

It didn't take much to work out that when matron over saw the preparations and did the rounds with Donald, the girls felt a lot better. However when left to his own devices, Donald was skimming some off the top. I also spied on him in his little office and saw him make up a package for collection on delivery days. I didn't have all the answers, which is why I spoke to Jenny Gill. I can't think of anything else to tell you."

Inspector Welford smiled. "You have knack for sniffing out drug dealers mister Beck, you ought to get a job with us. I will have to ask you to give us a written statement. One of my colleagues will be along later and deal with it."

Their refreshment arrived and the three sat quietly drinking coffee in silence.

Matron was first to speak. "Everybody here knew that Donald was a little strange, but he was good at his job. When I say strange, it was more that he was a little lecherous. He wasn't when he first came to us but after his wife left him, I'd see him staring at the women in here. I spoke with one of the consultants but they said it would only be a problem if it went any further, which as far as I am aware it never did. There were never any complaints made against him and his nursing and pharmaceutical skills were exemplary. I must shoulder some of the blame for this, as it happened under my supervision. I cannot see the board being too happy as it will have ruined the last few months trials of this new way of dealing with addiction."

The discussion continued for a short while until The Inspector made her apologies and after telling Jake she would be in touch, left for the police station. Jake followed her out and returned to the day room to reveal to Tina and Gail the days events.

Chapter 27

Jake spent another five weeks in the clinic before discharging himself. His consultant, Professor Johnson, tried to dissuade him, telling him that he knew Jake still had unresolved issues. He tried to convince Jake that time and talking about them would give him a better balance to his life. As far as Jake was concerned he had only one unresolved issue, and that was finding Nina's murderer. The professor even got Joseph to come and try to persuade him to give it a little more time, but to no avail. Before saying goodbye to The Aesculapius Clinic, he promised Tina and Gail that he would keep in touch and they exchanged telephone numbers.

"Mate, I'm no quack and if you think you should be back here at work, then I'm with you all the way. What frightens me is that you'll disappear again and these last few weeks have been in vain. We've been through a lot together and when I was at my lowest you were there for me. I will support you in any way I can, but you need to be honest with me, hell you need to be honest with all of us." Dave slapped Jake on the shoulder.

"Thanks Dave and I hear what you're saying. I will let you know if things get on top of me again. Believe it or not that stay in the clinic helped me sort lots of things out. There is only one problem left and that is Nina's death. I want the murdering bastard that killed her and I wont rest until I find him. I'm not asking you to get involved with that, but I can't let it drop. Enough said, I've been missing from here for too long so I have a bit of catching up to do. First I'm going to have a coffee, then I'm going to go over the books. You going to join me?"

Jake and Dave climbed the stairs to the office where they drank a coffee before Dave left to go to Earley to help Abe with installing a central heating system. As soon as Dave had left, Jake told Lisa he was going for a walk. Strolling quickly past Ian's premises, as he did not wish to discuss his stay in the clinic again today, he made his way to Jason's unit.

Jason saw him approaching and began to figure out what he was going to say if asked about any progress he had made regarding Nina's murder.

"Hi Jake. Nice to see you about again."

"Good to see you as well. You busy?"

"No. I've got a few minutes to spare if you want a coffee. I've even bought a machine the same as you and Ian have so you'll get a decent cup. Come on in and grab a pew."

Jason busied himself making the drinks, dreading what he knew was to come. He was not going to lie to Jake but he hoped that he would not have to tell all. Coffee brewed he carried the cups over and sat down.

Handing a cup to Jake he asked, "Is it okay to ask how you are?"

Jake laughed. "Course it is you silly sod. Not been the best time of my life but I feel okay. Still dark thoughts, but I'm learning to manage them. How about you, you good?"

For a while, they sat drinking and exchanging pleasantries, before Jake asked the one question that Jason was dreading. "Have you found out anything in relation to Nina's death?"

Jason looked directly at Jake. "I've been cringing at the thought of you asking me that question Jake. The simple answer is yes and no."

"It can't be both, either you've found something out or you haven't."

"Okay let me explain. I put out some feelers and asked someone a lot closer to this scene than me to make a few enquiries. He wound up in hospital having been badly beaten up."

"Bloody hell! Is he okay?"

"Yeah, he's okay. Sore but okay. I visited him in the hospital to find out what had happened. He says he was beaten up by Turks and so I called upon some unsavoury characters, I know to be caught up in the drug trade, to seek their assistance. As you can guess they didn't want to know. Well Shivers, that's the chap who was helping me out, is an ex para. Just like you I still have friends in the mob, especially those that were based in Aldershot, and with the help of friends of friends, a visit was paid to the Turks grill. I wasn't there, but I gather it was not pleasant, but the lads did manage to get the buggers to admit they were approached to help and gave the names of two thugs to a Dutchman. These Dutchmen are the new suppliers, having taken over from Riley. Trouble is I can't find a way to get hold of them. They appear and disappear. At the moment, I'm at a loss as to where to go next. There is a small chance that Omar, Ian's cousin Rupert, may be able to help, as he must get his supplies from these people. Last time we asked he didn't want to get involved, but a little bit of coercion may loosen his tongue."

"Jason you know these people better than I do, but I don't want anybody getting hurt on my behalf. To be honest I don't care too much for Omar, especially after he sent two of his cronies to do me over a few of years ago, so if it's possible to get something from him I won't worry so much."

*****

"I thought you said that we stay clear of Reading and only go there when its absolutely necessary." Joop enquired of Rudy.

"That's right, but this is necessary. Somebody is fucking with our deliveries and others are asking questions about two Dutchmen. I need to know what is going on. Still, you do not need to worry, I will sort it. You remember that park and restaurant where we went to see Cuza, take me there then go in and have yourself a lunch."

"On my own? What are you going to do?"

"That's right on your own, I have some personal business to deal with. Now, that's enough talking, just drive."

Their journey from the house they had rented, was across country and it took nearly forty-five minutes to reach the park. It had always been Rudy's opinion that you did not live near your business. As he often remarked 'you do not shit in your own nest'.

They parked up and both got out. Joop went in to the restaurant and Rudy climbed in the driving seat and drove off. Exiting the car park he found a space to park on the road, then switching off the engine he leaned back in his seat and lit a cigarette. He waited. About to light another cigarette there was a rapping on the rear window. Rudy could not figure out how he had missed somebody approach the Range Rover.

Rudy pushed the door release lock and two men climbed in to the back seats. Both were dressed in jeans and T-shirt with a grey hoodie jacket. There skin was the colour of Mediterranean types and both had beards. They were both carrying a sport bag.

"You are going to help us?" One of them spoke.

"Yeah I'll help you till the heat is off. All you two have to do is lie low until this trouble with the old man dies out. I have a place, it's not much as its due for demolition and redevelopment but it'll do you for a few weeks. It's a couple of miles from here. Have you got everything you want in those bags?"

"We have all we need here, although we will require extra food delivered. This would not be necessary if you had told us that *serseri* was army. We would not have let him seen us, or heard us. Now we have soldiers threatening to cut off our balls." The one who had spoken before was talking again and appeared to be the leader of the two.

"Look, it would have been better if you had killed the old sod. I really don't need this shit in my life, so you two just lay low until it blows over. Don't worry I'll give you a few quid to pay for your time, and what the fuck is a *serser*i?"

"You think we need it. We have families to care for. What are they going to think when we just disappear? I call that old man a *serseri* because he, what is it you say, down and out, street person."

"Right, so no one knows where are you, is that correct?"

"No. We have told no one."

Rudy started the Range Rover and drove out of Reading towards Pangbourne. Before he got to Purley, he turned left up an unmade track. The area looked as though it had been a chicken farm at some time in its history. He drove past what looked like sheds for battery hens, and further up a slope where a small, dilapidated bungalow came in to view. The windows were all boarded up, with a metal grille over them securely bolted in to the brickwork. Other than the chicken sheds there were no other buildings in sight.

"Right gentlemen this is where we get out." Rudy switched off the engine and stepped out. The two Turks joined him and they walked to the front door that had a steel plate fixed to it, and a large padlock securing entry.

Taking a key from his pocket, Rudy unlocked the door. "Here you had better have the key, but that is not an invitation for you to go outside. You stay in here until I say it is safe for you to return home. Got it?"

They entered the bungalow, which although covered in dust and cobwebs was at least dry. They walked through to the kitchen.

"Look in the fridge, its gas powered, because there is no electricity here, as is the cooker." As the one in front bent to look in the refrigerator, Rudy pulled a pistol from the waistband at the back of his trousers and putting the gun just behind the ear of the man in front of him pulled the trigger, filling the refrigerator with the front of his face.

The explosion caused the man at the refrigerator to jump up an start to turn, but before he was halfway up Rudy had shot him in the neck. He stared at Rudy as he continued turn with blood beginning to bubble from his mouth. Rudy shot him again through his eye. Blood, brain and splintered bone was spread across the walls and ceiling. He fell to the floor, joining his friend. Rudy bent down and plucked the key to the padlock from the Turks hand. He had no fear that anybody would have heard the gunshots. They were a good quarter of a mile off the road, and the bungalow and trees would have muffled the noise.

Rudy carefully padlocked the door behind him and climbed back in the Range Rover. It was just beginning to rain as he started the engine and turned on the wipers, thinking good luck was on his side. The rain would wash away any tyre tracks. Not that he was worried; no one ever came up here. He drove back to the road and towards the restaurant where he would pick Joop up. He liked Joop but he was to soft and would not approve of Rudy's way of cutting the ties of any thing that linked them to the old guy's assault.

Chapter 28

For the first time in a long time the group of friends were sat together in The Pond House. The only one who felt completely at ease was Jake. Even his mother felt she needed to tread on eggshells regarding what she said. For Lisa and Manda it was the first time they had been this close to someone who had gone through a mental breakdown. In the case of Abe, Alf, Ian, Dave and Jason they were trying to be careful about talking over old times and mentioning Nina's name Jake tried to ease the tension by raising his glass and toasting her memory as the absent wife and friend from the gathering.

It worked to some degree and the atmosphere relaxed a little, until that is Jake declared to all there that he intended to find out who had murdered Nina, and when he did, he would not be responsible for his actions. At this Pat burst in to tears and Alf told Jake he was a bloody fool. He understood how he felt but he should have had more regard for his mother. Furthermore if it wasn't for his precarious mental state he would have given him a good hiding. He and Pat left for home.

For a while after Alf and Pat had gone there was silence, then Dave spoke. "Alf was right Jake, you didn't need to come out with that in front of your mum. She's already worried sick about you."

Jake did not reply but Jason remarked, "You know we'll all help you where we can Jake, but we will not be party to you doing something stupid and ruining not only your life but the lives of those friends that care for you."

Jake muttered an apology and rose to go the bar. Jason and Ian followed him. Standing one each side of him Jason spoke first. "When you asked me to help you find out who could have been involved in Nina's death, I wasn't expecting you to go off the rails and in to a clinic for treatment. I realise that we must have rattled somebody's cage because of the beating that Shivers took. I'm trying to find out who the Dutchman is but that is difficult because no one is talking, or of course they're to damned scare to give his name. Omar won't play nicely and that means going back to the Turks for the two heavies that done Shivers over. Just the threat of a repeat visit from the soldier boys may be enough because I don't want to ask another favour of them. I'll try but I need you to promise me that you will not do anything stupid and you keep Ian and I in the picture."

Jake placed a hand on Jason's shoulder. "Thanks mate and you too Ian. You're doing more than it was fair to ask. I don't mean to upset people but this is eating away at me on the inside and I just can't let it rest."

*****

The three boys ran through the trees, pretending to chase and shoot a fleeing enemy. It did not matter too much the amount of noise they made, for they were far enough away from the road and any other inhabited property for them not to be heard.

The old sheds and three abandoned vehicles made it a perfect playground. They had of course been told by parents not go there and they ignored the *Private Keep Out* signs. Running out of steam they made there way to an old Ford saloon and sat in the ripped and torn seats.

Face still red from the exercise, a chubby boy called George, reached in to his jacket pocket and produced a packet of peanuts. "You two want some?" The other boys held out their hands.

Speaking through a mouthful of peanuts his friend called Timmy enquired, "What are we going to do now? My legs ache too much to keep running about."

"George's face lit up with a grin. "We are going down to the railway and see if there are any detonators in the hut. My old man used to nick a couple and drop bricks or he said fishplates on to 'em, to make 'em go off."

Chapter 29

Jason watched the takeaway. The lunchtime rush was coming to an end. It was another fifteen minutes before the shop was completely empty. He entered and threw the top bolt on the door and turned the sign to closed. Kaya watched him then picked up the telephone. Jason shook his head from side to side and indicated he should put the receiver down.

"I will ring the police if you do not leave now. Ishak told me to call them if you ever came back." Kaya had a worried look on his face, but he did replace the receiver. "He does not want any more trouble. Please go away, I do not know anything."

"You told my soldier friends that the man to ask for the names was Ali, a market trader. Well nobody knows this Ali. Now do I need to ask them to come back for the correct information or are you going to be sensible and tell me who they are." Kaya looked frightened and Jason was hopeful that he would give up the names. It was a while since he had needed to play the heavy, but in a perverse way, he found a small amount of pleasure in this revival of the old Jason.

Kaya feared the return of Jason's friends and he was also aware that Mehmet and Yunas had gone in to hiding and would remain there until it all blew over and the Dutchman said they could return home. Ishak was in Slough talking to a new meat supplier he was hoping to do business with. "If I give you the names you must promise that you did not hear them from me. If they find out, they will come for me and my family. They are not very nice men. You will do that?"

"I will forget I ever asked you."

You could see the fear in Kaya's eyes. "Their names are Mehmet and Yunas and they live in Zinzan Street. I do not know which house, but it is at the far end of the street. I think it is on the right hand side. They live there with their families. Now please go."

Jason turned to leave then stopped. "That had better be kosher, or I will be back."

*****

The blue telephone in Katrijn Spronk's began to ring. It rang six times and then gave the caller the message, voicemail, please speak. A voice said, "Thursday, zero six forty five ferry Rotterdam Harwich," and rang off.

*****

Joop sat in the armchair in the house in Aldershot. He could not put his finger on it, but over the last ten days, he felt that Rudy was not including him in everything. Like this new property development, he had mentioned. Joop did not expect to be asked if he wished to invest, but usually Rudy would have talked over any plans he had. Even when he went to visit the property, he had left him at the restaurant and gone on his own.

A door upstairs slammed and Rudy came down the stairs. "They're both up there if you want to spend a little relaxation time with them. They put on a great show together if you want. The blonde one does the most amazing things with her tongue, and that redhead bitch will make your eyes water."

"I'll forego the pleasure. I'm not in to eighteen year old tarts, prefer something with a little bit of flesh on it and some experience. Anyway isn't it a risk bringing girls back here. I thought this was supposed to be known to you and me only."

Rudy picked up his cigarettes and taking one from the pack, lit it, and drew the nicotine laden smoke deep in to his lungs. "Don't worry, they're so high on smack they'll never remember where this place is, Go on get upstairs and try some fresh young pussy."

Joop picked his jacket up from the back of a chair. "I'm going out for some fresh air."

Rudy watched him go and fell back in to an armchair. "Wanker," he mumbled, exhaling smoke in to the room. He sat quietly, finished one cigarette, and then lit another. His hand strayed to his groin and he considered going back upstairs for a repeat performance.

His mobile began to belt out *Rihanna's We Found Love*. He looked at the screen to find it was Sara. "Hi Sara, what do you want."

He sat up and moved the phone away from his ear as she screamed, "I want to know what the fuck is going on. That is another delivery and driver grabbed by customs. Some fucker is passing on information and I want to know who."

"I don't fucking believe this. Some bastard is playing us for silly buggers. Apart from Cuza, you and me nobody had any knowledge of this load. I'm going to start asking questions this end and you need to the same over there. How about De Groot is he okay?"

"Niels is fine. He doesn't have any knowledge of delivery dates or routes. He is arranging for the driver to be offered financial security for keeping his mouth shut."

"Okay so it's not De Groot. Can he get one of his unsavoury friends to make a few discreet enquiries. I would look particularly close at Cuza. In the meanwhile Sara we both need to rack our brains and think who else it may be."

"I'll ask him. I know you don't like Cuza, but I'm sure it's not him. We'll see what Niels can turn up, and if Cuza gets a clean bill of health, then I'll get him to look at the Romanian end. Keep in touch."

Chapter 30

The bungalow was cordoned off with police tape, as was the track from the road to the buildings. There were two Scenes of Crime vans, two marked and three unmarked police cars.

A young female officer was being comforted by a male colleague, having been violently sick, just outside of the cordon.

"She alright?" a sergeant enquired.

A man of about forty dressed in jeans, polo shirt, and an olive green leather jacket looked from the sergeant and then across to their female workmate. "She will be. Bit tough, this being her first body, especially one that's a few days old that's been feasted on by rats and is riddled with maggots. I remember my first one. Now, if when I enter a building and I can hear the buzz of flies, I cover my mouth and nose with a hanky that has either olbas oil or Vicks vapour rub on it."

The sergeant grimaced, then looked back at his senior officer, Detective Superintendent Cameron McArthur. "Eh sir, bad enough when they die and just vent their bowels. When half the head is missing from the gunshot and some of the flesh is moving with maggots, it's a real bummer. Christ knows how those kids reacted. It's a large area so I will leave four of mine with you and radio for some more for a thorough search of the area."

Taking off his leather jacket and throwing it on the passenger seat of an unmarked Ford Mondeo McArthur walked towards a woman dressed from head to toe in a pale blue forensic suit. "Anything you can tell me Jill?"

Jill Martin was a forensic pathologist. She wore no make up and her attire would let a person learn very little, covered as she was from head to toe. Jill was forty two, blonde with an athletic figure verging on skinny. "Difficult to be precise but I estimate ten days. Body A was shot from behind the left ear, from very close range, which removed the anterior portion of the skull it is almost completely blown away. This would have caused death but until I can get the body on the table and opened up, I can't tell you a lot more. Body B has more than one gunshot wound but again I need to open him up to tell you much more."

The detective grunted, then told both Jill and the sergeant he was returning to his office. Although he was the SIO, senior investigating officer, DCI Ted Potter would be the man running the show on the ground. McArthur took one last look around then walked purposely back to his car

"Oh well sarge, in that case I can expect a call two minutes after I've got back to the lab, asking if I have the results of the autopsy. Never one too hang about is Ted."

"No, he does tend to be in a hurry with life. You'd have thought at his age he would start to slow down a little." Sergeant Willis smiled at Jill. "Well, I'm also going back to the factory. I need to find some bodies to do a search of the area. Trouble is it's been so long and those boys have been running amok through the grounds and forcing entry to the property, that I doubt there's much to find. See you again Doc."

Jill set off to find Ted Potter. There was nothing more she could do here. The SOCO guys and gals were painstakingly taking pictures and examining every inch of the property. Luckily some bright bobby had noticed the lock on the door was new and it was still in place, securing the front door. The young boys swore they had not touched it but McArthur had said he doubted that as in his words the little sods would have tried every window and door. She would ask Ted Potter if he agreed that the bodies could be removed to the mortuary.

*****

True to his word, Jason told Jake about the two Turks, Mehmet and Yunas, and together they visited Zinzan Street. It did not take long for them to discover which house they lived in. It seemed the two lived together along with their wives and five kids.

All to no avail as the wives reluctantly told them they had no idea where their husbands were and both Jason and Jake believed them.

"Sorry Jake. Just as I thought we were getting somewhere, we seem to have come to another dead end."

"Not quite Jason, we can still go back to that market trader. He must know something."

"Nobody knows this Ali. I think it was just a name Osman passed on to get me off his back. Still he gave us these two so maybe a little more pressure can be applied."

The two set off for the takeaway and on entering the premises they could see the fear on Kaya Osman's face.

Kaya soon spilt the beans on how he had given Jason the two names, because a day or so previously Mehmet had called for a kebab and let slip that the Dutchman had found somewhere for them lie low for a while. He did not know where.

Chapter 31

"Rudy, I need to know what the hell is going on. We've lost two loads and now Cuza is threatening to stop supplies. He is worried that sooner or later the police will work backwards and find where they come from. This would finish us as by the time we find a new supplier we will have lost our dealers. Something is fucking wrong and we need to find out fast. The only people that know are Cuza, me and you. Cuza has convinced me that it is not him, which leaves you and me. I have got to ask you this Rudy, but are you trying to screw me."

"Sara I have screwed you once and as pleasant an experience that was, I am not looking to repeat it in any form. There is of course Joop, but he doesn't know the delivery details until a few days later when we collect the payments. Drugs and cash are never exchanged on the same day. For one bust it could be that the police were lucky, but two, never."

"Likewise this end. The money is passed through the hotels and the market stalls businesses that are set up for that purpose. The cash never reaches here until ten or more days later so I don't see that being a problem."

In order to launder the money, Sara had three hotels. Not so much your regular hotel, but a slap house where rooms were rented by the hour and payment for this type of business was usually cash. Her hotels were extremely busy! The market stalls that traded along the side of the canals were popular with tourists and again turnover was predominantly cash.

Hearing the door to the apartment being opened, Sara told Rudy she would have to go, but would call him later.

Viona entered the bedroom. "Who were you on the phone to? Was it a restaurant or a club for tonight?"

Sara snapped. "No it fucking wasn't. It was an old friend of my brothers who now spends most of his time in England"

Sara had never spoken to Viona like that before and she was visibly shocked. Sara noticed this and stepped towards her and gave her a hug. "Sorry Vee, but we were talking about Max and I got a little upset recalling what used to be. I shall make it up to you. Choose wherever you want to go tonight and I shall arrange it. Come, I need a shower and as you have been out shopping all morning, I guess you do too. We will shower together and ensure our bodies are extremely clean. I love the way you soap and caress me and then we can go to bed before going out tonight."

*****

"That was you wasn't it? You fucking killed them. What the hell are you doing? We are supposed to be living a nice quiet life here, keeping our heads down, and keeping the business ticking over. You have to go round murdering people which will only involve the police starting a hunt for their killer. Are you fucking mad or something. I'm beginning to wonder if I need to be connected to all this. I vowed that I would not go back inside, and this although risky meant good money for little effort, but accessory to murder, I don't need this kind of crap." Joop was waving his arms around and pacing about the room.

Rudy lay back in his armchair, cigarette in hand. "Joop my friend you worry too much, No I am not mad, I am tidying up a few loose ends which could come back to haunt us. The police will find nothing to tie me to that place, I left it as clean as a whistle. I trust Ishak, so we are back where we were at the beginning."

"Of course we're not. Too begin with, we had nobody looking for us, now the police are investigating three murders and an assault. You call that nothing."

*****

Jake had dropped in on Jason on his way to his unit. "That's another dead end. Whoever murdered the Turks is cleaning up behind themselves. My money is on the Dutchmen. Any ideas where we go next?"

Jason shook his head. "Not at the moment, but I'll give it some thought. You want a coffee?"

Agreeing a coffee would be good, they made their way to back of the garage.

Chapter 32

Ted Potter knocked on Superintendent McArthur's and heard the shout to enter.

"I know you're busy Ted but I'm wondering if you have any further progress to report on the murders of those Turks. I'm being pressed by the ACC who has the press and the Turkish Association on his back."

"Sorry sir, but I am going to be of little help. The crime scene is an absolute mess, what with those kids treating it as a playground. The rain last week would have washed away any tyre marks, but maybe a small glimmer of hope. A new padlock was fitted and it seems you cannot purchase it in this country. I have one of my researchers trying to discover where they can be purchased. Also, although the padlock and hasp and staple had been wiped clean, we are hoping the perp hadn't realised he'd touched the covered plate and left a partial print. Course it might not be his because we haven't found a match, but because of the padlock we forwarded the print to Interpol. I've asked DC Newman to chase them up. I hope that they will come up with a name. Meanwhile we plod on."

"Thanks Ted. I'll let you get back to the troops."

Ted wandered back to his own office, stopping to shout to Zoe to get him a coffee and bring it to his office.

*****

"Joop, pack a bag we're going on holiday. In order to put your mind at rest we will go away for a while."

"Who is going to look after things back here? You can't just up sticks and move abroad, even if only for a short while."

"Sara is sending someone over to keep an eye on things. Anyway, we'll only be a couple of hours away. We're going golfing on the Costa del Sol."

"Do you know who Sara is sending over? She's not trying to get us out and someone new in is she?"

For a moment Rudy was speechless, but quickly gathering his thoughts he replied, "No. It was my idea for us to get away. She said she knew someone who would step in and keep an eye on things while we're in Spain. I've known Sara too long for her to double cross me. Max and me went back a long way." Rudy lit his cigarette then said. "I'll be able to get some cheap fags over there. The prices here are fucking unbelievable."

"Get packed we need to be at Gatwick in a few hours. I've got an old friend meeting us at Malaga and he's found us an apartment to use." Rudy laughed then broke in to the seventies hit *Y Viva Espana* by *Sylvia Vrethammar.*

*****

Sara had been waiting at Schipol airport for Eric Cuza's flight from Bucharest. The flight was delayed and she cursed for not having checked arrival times on the internet before making the journey. Eric was here for one night only. He did not like being outside of his homeland, where he had enough officials on his bankroll to ensure his safety. After the loss of two deliveries, he was concerned and insisted on a face-to-face meeting with Sara. He was also going to introduce Sara to his man in Amsterdam, the man who would look after the UK end of the business for a couple of weeks or so, while Rudy and Joop took a break in Spain. It was fortuitous that Rudy had suggested the vacation. It saved any ill feeling if Eric had insisted on having his man run an eye over Rudy's running of the set up.

Nearly fifty minutes late, Eric appeared in the Arrivals lounge. Following a quick embrace, they walked through to the car park and Sara's car. Eric asked her to take him to the Grand Amsterdam.

Eric always stayed there when in Amsterdam. It was expensive but he considered it, money well spent. Why, they even provided a personal butler service. The location was magnificent. The monumental buildings between two canals had served as a 15th-century convent, the headquarters of the Dutch Admiralty in the Golden Age, the Town Hall and even the site of the current Queen Beatrix's wedding reception in 1966. Eric loved the opulence.

He told Sara to come up to his room so that they could discuss what his man, Ruud Van Winkel, would be doing, and to introduce him to her. He would call him and arrange for the three of them to have a meal that evening. Sara agreed but suggested they meet an hour before the meal so that her girlfriend, Viona, could join them for the meal. She explained that she owed her tonight and this would solve the problem. Eric agreed provided she was not included in the prior discussion and not one word of their business was part of the dialogue during the meal.

Chapter 33

The morning briefing had begun at seven thirty. Disappointingly, there was nothing new to report and nothing to point them in the right direction. Ted ran over what each member of his team was to concentrate on, but inwardly felt sorry for them, as even he could see they had absolutely nothing. A big fat Zero.

DS Jim Calhoun was coordinating and his whiteboard that should have shown what they had learnt looked pretty bleak. Jim was a stickler for rules and was regimented in his approach, but it worked very well for managing the information as it was received.

The padlock although not available in the UK was widely available in most of Europe. They were still awaiting a reply from Interpol in respect of the partial fingerprint.

Before winding the meeting up Ted asked Andrea Thorowgood, a DC, if she had heard from Jill Fraser. She told him no, and Ted said he would telephone her after he had been to report their lack of progress to Superintendent McArthur and had a coffee.

Having reported the sorry state of affairs to the Superintendent, he called out to Zoë to fetch him a coffee. Ted phoned Jill Fraser and was told she was unavailable for the next hour. Deciding he would do a spot of legwork he told Jim Calhoun where he was going and left for the town centre with DC Newman. Zoe Newman was both new to his team, and Reading. Zoe was university educated and had a knack of thinking outside the box.

Introducing Zoe to the delights of various local pubs and their clientele, they were enjoying a soft drink in the Red Cow when a dishevelled looking character entered the bar. With a good weeks growth of beard and clothes that had charity stamped all over them the man made his way to the bar.

"A pint please." He began extracting coins from his pocket and counting them out on the bar.

"You can have a pint Seamus and when you've finished it, you're to be on your way. This isn't a drop in centre for waifs and strays." The landlady was a bottle blonde and her drawn features gave her an anorexic look.

Rising from his seat, Ted indicated that Zoe should remain where she was. He approached the bar and stood next to Seamus. "Not seen you around in a while Seamus."

A Dish Best Served Cold

Turning to see who had spoken to him Seamus took a step back. A grin spread across his face. "Why it's you Mister Potter. I'd buy you a drink but unfortunately my budget doesn't stretch that far."

"Nice that you should have the thought Seamus. But we will have a drink and I will buy you one."

"That's most kind of you; can I have a Jamesons to help this on its way?"

Ted indicated to the landlady, who had been watching and listening to their exchange, to bring him a whiskey. As she put it on the bar Seamus made to pick it up. Before his hand reached it, Ted had covered the glass with his own palm. "In a minute Seamus, first I want to pick your brain."

"You know I will help you if I can, but I don't know anything."

"I haven't asked the question yet Seamus. Now you are friends with the Turks."

"Not exactly friends, but they sometimes give me a kebab, as long as I move away from the shop to eat it. Some of the others will drop me a few coins. They're nice people Mister Potter."

"That's right Seamus, and as you will have heard, two of them were murdered. I want to know who carried out these killings, and I'm hoping you can help me. What's the word on the street. Who is behind this Seamus?"

"I honestly don't know. If I did I would tell you." The landlady's ears were still pricked up. Lowering his voice Seamus whispered, "Saint Giles church in five minutes."

"Okay Seamus you can have your drink. I was hoping that maybe you would know something. If you do hear anything, let me know."

Finishing his pint and whiskey chaser, Seamus left the bar. Nearly ten minutes later, Ted said to Zoe, loud enough for the landlady to hear, that there was nothing more there for them and they should return to the station.

Chapter 34

Arriving back at the station DC Andrea Thorowgood told him that Jill Fraser had called a couple of times saying she had something important to tell him. Ted pulled his mobile from his pocket only to discover the battery was flat. It had happened a few times of late and he made a mental note to replace either the battery or more probably the mobile itself. He walked through to his office and after checking the stick-its, that were plastered over his screen, and giving a cursory glance at two new files that had been placed on his desk, he sat down, and dialled Jill Fraser's number.

She answered almost immediately. Pleasantries were exchanged and Ted asked, "Have you been trying to get hold of me? I must apologise, my battery was flat."

"Yeah, I have some news that may help you with this Turkish case. You have the autopsy reports but what you won't know is that the gun that killed these two was used to kill a woman in Riseley. I dealt with her autopsy and you need to contact DI Joe Hopkins who was dealing with the case. I don't know if this is any help or not because Joe's case is still unsolved."

"Whatever, it means that this person has killed again and if we look carefully we should find a clue somewhere to lead us to them." Ted interceded.

Jill continued. "The bullets are point four five calibre from a SIG Sauer P227 as far as the forensic people can ascertain. A real hard-hitting weapon. Well that's my news for today. I'll let you know if anything else turns up."

Ted was digesting this information when Zoe Newman knocked on his door and opened it just wide enough to stick her head in. "Good news sir. Interpol have given us a name for the fingerprint. Ronald Smit. They are faxing a copy of the file because he also uses a number of aliases. I will bring it to you as soon as it is received."

Ted thanked Zoe then picked up his desk phone and dialled Superintendent McArthur's number. He waited for McArthur to answer then asked if it was convenient for him to see him.

Two minutes later, he was seated in Macarthur's office, bringing him up to date with the new information received.

McArthur sat deep in thought for a couple of minutes. Ted could see he was thinking and sat quietly, not interrupting.

McArthur spoke. "Joe Hopkins is running the Nina Beck case. Like you, he has found it difficult to make any progress and the matter is on the back burner. If you're agreeable and he's happy, then I will ask him to hand over to you. I can't see him complaining, he's got enough on his plate with the town centre stabbings of those two young black girls. One has died this morning so he now has a murder on his hands. Bloody senseless, and all over some boy. Sit tight Ted, I'll see if he's in his office."

Less than five minutes passed before there was a tap on the door and DI Joe Hopkins entered. There followed a short discussion where Joe Hopkins agreed that it was wise to transfer ownership of the case to Ted. Joe's own thoughts were that it was destined to be a cold case at a future date. Another bonus was that he would not receive a weekly call from Jake Beck asking if any progress had been made. He did not consider the calls a nuisance but found it difficult to tell a man whose wife had been murdered, that there was no change.

*****

Eric looked at Sara. "Ruud has already arranged a new driver, and he will no longer inform Rudy the date of shipping. Tomorrow he will go to Reading and check out the arrangements in place over there."

The meeting had gone better than Sara expected. They did not order food, but Eric and Ruud had beers while Sara ordered a bottle of Krug. They would eat when Viona joined them. When Eric had told her they needed to meet, she had thought the worst. Losing two loads and two drivers in such a short time could not be put down to the vigilance of some customs officer, after all their route through Rotterdam was paid for. Bribery did not come cheap. At least Eric did not suspect her or that the problem was in Holland, although all evidence pointed that way. It was felt that Ruud would quietly have a word with all their dealers and let it be known that if they, their lieutenants, or soldiers were found to be the culprits, then a speedy and painful solution would be implemented. Sara agreed that the plan was sensible and had no objections to Ruud questioning her people.

Ruud Van Winkel was a man in his thirties, blonde-haired, about five feet ten inches. He was broad shouldered but narrow at the hips. A scar ran from the left side of his forehead down across his cheek, the cut having passed over the eye socket, but missing the eyeball itself. The injury was slightly masked by his pock marked face.

Every time he looked at Sara she felt another layer of clothes was being removed. The way he leered at her and his scarred face frightened her, and there were not many people that scared her.

The meeting over, Viona joined them. Sara gave her a full on kiss for Ruud's benefit and out of the corner of her eye she could see the smile that crept across Eric's face.

Chapter 35

"It's been two weeks and we have bugger all to go on." Ted Potter looked around the incident room. Cases like this led to despondency amongst the team. "Right, we need to get a foothold on this enquiry so Andy, I'd like you and Andrea to go back over any cases involving Turks for the past six months, and if you find nothing, go back another six months." This brought a groan from Ted's DS, Andy Jones. "Sorry Andy and you Andrea but we need something to kick start this enquiry."

Turning his attention towards Zoe he said, "Zoe I want you to phone all local hotels, B and B's, letting agents, you know what I want, and go through the list of aliases that this Ronald Smit uses to see if he has booked a room locally in the last twelve month. Before you start that a coffee please." He turned and looked at a DC sat away in the corner, doodling on a piece of paper, "And you Ryan can help her." Another groan. "Right, get to it ladies and gentleman, and I use that description very loosely."

Ted remained in the incident room until Zoe returned with his coffee, and then returned to his office. It was still only eight thirty in the morning. Logging in on his computer, he checked the e-mails that had come in overnight. Requests for overtime sheets, expense claims, reports on various team members, budget forecasts, but nothing representing detective work. There was a tap on the door and Zoe poked her head around it. "I've just taken a call from a Kevin Hutt asking to have a word with somebody dealing with the Turks case. Doesn't want to talk on the phone but says he will be home this pm if somebody could pop round. Says he can't come in 'cos he's looking after grandchildren."

"Does it sound promising from what he's told you?"

"Well he knows something but how relevant it will be, I couldn't say. DS Jones says he will take me unless you want to go. His words were we've got fuck all now so we won't be losing anything by listening to him."

"No, you and Andy sort it. I will be spending the day in my office in my role as accountant, researcher, analyst, clairvoyant and any other job that those upstairs can think of to keep me from being a detective." Also on his desk was the file on Nina Beck's murder. There was no chance he would find time today to read it. "Ah well," he thought, "another night spent at home trying to catch up on the days work. Cathy his wife would be well pleased. She was always reminding him that he had a wife at home who once in a while would be glad of his company.

A Dish Best Served Cold

Zoe gave him a quizzical look and returned to her desk.

*****

"Any luck finding out how we can track down these Dutch guys, or better still an address.

Jason looked disconsolate as he answered Jake. "Sorry Jake, but not a thing. People know there are a couple of Dutchmen around and that they are responsible for the drugs that have become available again, but nobody knows where too find them. We can't even be sure that they have anything to do with Nina's murder, after all their interest will be drugs, not a nursing sister. The only chance is the Turk. Perhaps I'll have another word with him."

"Don't be disappointed Jason, we've, or I should say you, have done your best. I couldn't ask for more. Nobody is talking and there's not much more we can do to make them. Come on I'll buy you a pint. That's the vey least you deserve."

"I'd be grateful for that, and Jake I haven't given up on something turning up. May be I'm too long out of the game. Christ I even had to call on a favour from old army buddies to deal with the Turks, when a few years back I'd have walked in that grill and just the threat of breaking a few skulls would have got me the answers."

"If there's one thing I don't want you doing is placing yourself at risk of arrest on my behalf. I mean it Jason, no risk to your well-being. Come on the pub'll be closed by the time we get there."

Charlie Gardner

*****

Zoe and Andy drove out to Arborfield. Finding the house they required they knocked on the door.

It was answered by a stockily built man in his fifties. "Hi, you must be the police. Come in. You'll have to excuse me but I've only been in a little while. Sorry about the smell but I've just cooked myself an all day breakfast."

DS Jones produced his warrant card. "Mister Kevin Hutt? I'm DS Jones and this is DC Newman."

"Yeah. I'm Kevin Hutt. Come on through."

They walked through a hallway to a sitting room where a young girl was sat at the table both doing a jigsaw and playing with a doll. When the piece of the jigsaw did not fit, it was the dolls fault.

Kevin sat at the table where his half-eaten meal was getting cold. The aroma of the fried smoked bacon set Andy's mouth watering.

After the offer of a cup tea which they politely refused, Kevin told his story in between mouthfuls of food and a slurp of tea.

He had been doing a job for a friend who owned some houses in Zinzan Street. He was finishing off, and loading his tools in to his van when a Range Rover pulled in front. He called out that he would be going in a few minutes and that they had left him scant room to manoeuvre out of his space. The passenger gave him a menacing look as he began to get out and told him to piss off. Before it could go any further, his mate grabbed him by the arm and told him to leave it. They were both foreigners and at a guess, he reckoned they were Dutch. In his younger days, he had spent a few weekends in Amsterdam and got used to the accent.

"Very interesting Mister Hutt, but what help is that to us?" Andy butted in.

"Well the house they knocked on the door of was the one where those two blokes who got murdered lived. When one the wives answered the door, they just barged in. They were only in there for a few minutes, 'cos I was still loading when they came out. The passenger called out to me that I should be more polite in future. His mate the driver called out for him to get in the Range Rover, as they had to be off. He called him Rudy and said they had to get back to Aldershot."

Zoe had been taking notes and said, "Are you sure that is what he said? Did you get the reg number of the vehicle?"

"I am one hundred per cent certain and I will not forget the bastard who threatened me. Next time I'll give him a chance to take a swing at me." Kevin paused for a mouthful of tea. "I did jot down the reg number but I cannot find the piece of paper I scribbled it on anywhere. Sorry but if I come across it I'll give you a buzz."

"Well mister Hutt you just be glad that you didn't get in to a fight with this man, because the chances are he would have killed you." Andy remarked.

Kevin was asked to clarify one or two points, during which Zoe's mobile started chirping. She apologised for the interruption. Zoe finished talking to Kevin and then offered her apologies while she went outside to answer her mobile that was ringing again. Zoe returned to the sitting room where Andy was winding up the interview. Andy gave him a card with his office and mobile number on it.

Back at the office, Zoe could not wait to get back on the telephone.

Chapter 36

"Digame."

"Stop pissing about Rudy, you've got a problem." Sara did not sound amused at Rudy's attempt to answer his mobile in Spanish.

"What is my problem now. I am over here at Puerto Capobina in the sunshine surrounded by bars and pretty senoritas. Life is good."

"Shut up for a minute you fool and listen to what I have to say. The DNR (Dienst Nationale Recherche - Dutch National Police Force.) have sent a copy of your file to the British police. They must be on to you. You need to disappear, and not to Spain where the English keep a watchful eye. South America or Eastern Europe, Russia even."

Rudy interrupted. "Hold on a minute. What do they know? Who told you this? I have heard nothing from my source in Reading."

The source is impeccable. An officer in the Dutch force is on Eric's payroll and passed the information to him."

"Cuza! I wouldn't trust that Romanian gypsy as far as I could throw him. He wants me out and this is his way of doing it. He's trying to panic you Sara. Ignore it, I am." Rudy drew deeply on his cigarette then exhaled loudly.

There was silence whilst Sara thought over what Rudy had said. Was Cuza trying to take over their distribution in Southern England? She trusted Rudy one hundred per cent and although her relationship with Cuza was good, she had only known him for just over eighteen months. He already had his man Ruud Van Winkel in place in Reading. Did she really know what he was up to? She rang off but not before telling Rudy to be careful.

Joop had been sat in a chair supping a beer. Rudy turned to him, "Joop my friend, I think we have a problem. We may have to return to England." Rudy went on to explain what Sara had told him.

Joop listened to what Rudy had to tell him then finishing his beer he said he was off to pack his case. "Well whether it's Brazil or the UK, I shall be ready. One thing for certain, I can't see us remaining here."

*****

Zoe tapped on Ted's door and entered on a grunted reply.

"Guv, I've been on the phone chasing up lettings in Aldershot and think I may have a lead on our Dutch pair."

Aldershot? Where did that come from?"

"When we interviewed Kevin Hutt he mentioned over hearing one of them say they had to get back to Aldershot. On the off chance I chased around letting agents asking if they had let any properties to Dutchmen over the past couple of years and hey presto one has just called and says a colleague let a property just over eighteen months to someone called Rudolf Smit, one of Aken's known aliases. I am faxing over a face shot to see if the colleague, Roger Smith, can confirm that it is our man."

"Well done Zoe. If this turns out well I'll make sure you get the credit for it. Keep me up to date 'cos if necessary we'll have to liaise with Hampshire to keep an eye on the place. Meanwhile do me a favour and fetch me a coffee, with a double shot, I need it this afternoon."

The following day Roger Smith telephoned to say he was ninety per cent sure that the photo was of the man he had let the house to. Unfortunately, there was no card or cheque transaction to follow up on as the deal was completed in cash and the rent was paid six months in advance on the dot. It was enough for Ted and he asked Superintendent McArthur to contact his counterpart in Aldershot and make the necessary arrangements.

Superintendent Chris Collins of Hampshire Constabulary called McArthur back an hour later and said he had two men watching the property but he expected McArthur to provide two members of his own team before shift change that evening. As an aside, he mentioned that it appeared there was no one present at the property. McArthur let Ted Potter know and told him to get it organised.

Ted rose from his chair, strode to his office door which he opened, and stuck his head in to the corridor. "DC Newman, my office, pronto." He called out.

A moment later Zoe appeared and he informed her what had been agreed between Hampshire and McArthur. She and DS Jones were to take over surveillance of the property in Aldershot until eight o'clock tomorrow morning when DC's Thorowgood and Collins would relieve them. Jones was out on an enquiry but would return in about twenty minutes. He suggested they try to get some rest before leaving to take up their observation.

At seven forty five that evening they were ensconced in an unmarked van, keeping a watchful eye on the house in Alexandra Road that Rudolf Smit had rented.

Chapter 37

There had been no sighting of the Dutchmen overnight and Zoe and Andy had taken it in turns to grab a few minutes sleep. There was a light tap on the door, and Andy moved across and opened it. Andrea and Ryan quickly stepped in to the van bringing with them the smell of coffee and the delicious aroma of fried smoked bacon.

Zoe gave them a smile. "That's very kind of you to turn up early, we're both absolutely shattered. Have you got coffees in that bag you're carrying?"

"Sorry," Ryan said, looking all-apologetic, "We only bought the two for us."

"Fucking great!" exclaimed Andy. "Stuck here all bloody night and you don't even think to bring us a hot coffee."

"Christ sarge, you're so bloody easy to wind up. Yeah we got you coffees and a bacon roll." Andrea laughed and the scowl on Andy's face softened.

In between sips of coffee and mouthfuls of bacon roll Andy explained that nobody had approached or entered the property and no lights had been switched on or off during the evening and night time. The place looked empty.

After Andy and Zoe had departed, Andrea made a call to the letting agents and asked what power company provided the electricity for the property. The young girl the other end of the line gave her the account number and full details of the supplier. Andrea gave them a call. A few minutes later, she told Ryan she was off to the shops.

Ryan continued to watch the street and after a short while spotted Andrea walking towards the property then walk up to a plastic box mounted on the wall by the front door. Producing a plastic tool from her pocket, she inserted it into a hole in the box and twisted it, releasing the front panel. She looked in the box and jotted down something in her notebook. Shutting the front panel on the box, she returned to the surveillance vehicle.

"What was that all about? What did you find in that box?" Ryan enquired.

"Nothing that shouldn't have been there. The house is empty."

Andrea called the DCI and told him what she had discovered. He told her to stay where they were and

A Dish Best Served Cold

he would arrange for a search team, and a warrant. Meanwhile he would ask the letting agents for a set of keys so that they would not have to batter the door down.

Two hours later, there was two squad cars plus two unmarked cars and a Scenes of Crime forensic vehicle outside the property. A thorough search was being carried out.

The DCI pulled Andrea to one side. "That was clever thinking Andrea. We could have spent days here waiting for something to happen. At least now, we can search the premises and see if we can pick up a lead. After all we have bugger all else."

"Thanks Guv. It only came to me this morning as I had a card put through my door telling me to phone the electric company if I wished to provide actual meter reading rather than an estimated one. My meter is inside the hall cupboard so they can't read it unless I'm there to let them in. Saw the meter box on the wall and when a neighbour told me the meters were read two weeks ago, I just thought it might be an idea to check usage."

A uniformed officer interrupted them. "Thought you would be interested in this sir." He handed a scrap of paper to the DI who straightened out the crinkles and studied the document.

Ted called Andy over. "It's been a long day and I suggest we begin to wind up here and resume tomorrow. The buggers are in Spain and have an open ticket, so they could return any time. I've informed immigration who will let us know the minute they appear. We'll finish up here tomorrow, then wait for our holiday makers to return. Surveillance can remain in place, but when we leave tomorrow, it must look as if we've never been here. I'm off back to the nick if you want me."

*****

Although Jake had given up on finding the two Dutchmen, he still felt the need to ask Jason if he had been able to get any more information from the Turk.

"I called at the grill and saw Kaya. Reckons himself tough but when I mentioned that my army friends were enquiring after Shivers health, you could see the fear in his eyes. He's given me two names, only Christian names but says he doesn't know where to find them. They always call here and Ishak is the one with their mobile number. After that, I went to see Omar and he has confirmed the names and says his only means of contact is a mobile. The one thing he did say was that he was sure they had somebody in this area who is their ears and eyes."

"What makes him think that?"

"Well as soon as something is not quite right, Rudy soon appears. I didn't expect anything from Omar, but reading between the lines, he is not feeling so safe with the Dutchmen around. The word on the street is that they either killed or had somebody kill the two Turks. Maybe Omar fears for his own life. He mentioned that a while ago there was a bit of a fracas in the Turks restaurant. Rudy is a bit of a loose cannon."

Jake had a smile on his face. "I honestly thought that you would have nothing to tell me tonight Jason. Okay we haven't got much but we have a damned sight more than we did last week. A few years ago, we were the opposite sides of the fence, but at the moment, although I have some very good friends, I put my trust in you. Maybe it's because you can understand the situation, whereas the others would tell me to keep away from it. Whatever, I do appreciate your help."

Jason adopted a serious look. "Bloody hell Jake you'll have me shedding a tear in a minute. Just answer me one question honestly. Well two actually. Are you on medication or do you still suffer with dark thoughts? Also what do you intend to do if you catch up with these Dutchmen?"

Jake thought for a moment then said, "That's three questions. Am I depressed? Yes, and I don't know when it will end, well I do, it's when the bastards who killed Nina are dead. And no, I am not taking any medication."

"Wow Jake hold on a minute. You know there's no death sentence so that's unlikely to happen. Don't tell me you're even thinking of exacting your own revenge on them."

"If I'm honest Jason it scares me what I might do if I had the pair of them at my mercy."

Chapter 38

Andy took a careful look at the photographs in his hands and the room he was stood in. He had made a scrupulous inspection of each room to ensure it was just as they had found them prior to the search. The search had been thorough and investigators had been painstaking in ensuring that drawers had been left in the condition they were to start with. No weapon had been found and the Armed Response Vehicle was still outside.

He nodded to Zoe to indicate they could now vacate the premises. The Dutchmen were due back tomorrow. He crossed the road to the ARV and told them they could now resume their normal patrol.

Joop turned in to and drove slowly along Alexandra Road, but as they approached the property Rudy suddenly sat up in his seat and said, "Keep going. Don't accelerate, just drive on by."

A Dish Best Served Cold

Joop done as instructed, and asked, "What's up?"

"That bloke by that police car, I'm sure he came from our house. Keep going, we won't be coming back."

"Where to?"

"Not sure yet but just get away from here. I need to think."

The pair set off towards Farnham. After a while Rudy punched a number in to his mobile. There followed a short conversation with Rudy explaining to someone the other end their predicament. A prolonged conversation ensued. Finishing the call, he turned to Joop. "Right, we're going to Tidmarsh."

"Where the hell is Tidmarsh. Never heard of it."

"And neither had I until a few minutes ago. I have a postcode; I'll enter it in the sat nav."

It took over an hour travelling across country to find the house in Tidmarsh. Surrounded by a two-metre wall with tall Leylandi trees behind, it was well hidden, and the house could not be seen from the road. Large wrought iron gates barred their access. Rudy gave Joop a number to punch in to the keypad. As they drove in the drive curved to the left and brought in to view a modern bungalow and a three-car garage.

"Nice pad," said Joop, "Who does it belong to?"

"A company registered in the Caymans. Ultimately, it belongs to Sara, but she has only visited twice. It won't be much inside as it's not lived in and we'll have to get some grocery if we want to eat and drink. The good thing is there's some stables round the rear and a track that leads on to a back lane that goes cross-country to Tilehurst. Pull in round the back and I'll find the key, It's above a beam in the middle stable."

The moment they entered the house they could tell no one had lived there for at least a year. Furniture was sparse which led to Joop to remark that this must be what they describe as minimalist. Joop proceeded to pull the dust covers off a couple of armchairs.

Rudy went upstairs to investigate the bedrooms and familiarise himself with the layout of the house. He returned to the living room where Joop was stretched out on a sofa. "You get a good view of the road and surrounding area from the upstairs and one of the bedrooms has a balcony at the back. Easy enough to jump from and get away if we have too. We'll leave the Range Rover at the back all the time, just in case."

Joop snapped back. "There wouldn't be a 'just in case' if you hadn't topped those Turks. They wouldn't have talked and even if they had, they didn't know enough. We're holed up here 'cos you fucked up."

Rudy gave Joop a hard stare and the finger. He walked behind the sofa Joop was laying on and lit a cigarette. "I do what I have to do to protect me. Anybody gets in my way, then I deal with it. I'm going to walk back to the village pub and get a few bottles, and I need some fags."

Joop sprang up off the sofa. "There you go again. You don't think. You want fags and booze so you'll go down the local pub in a village. No we'll find some shop out of the way so that people don't recognise us. Go to the pub and the locals will think we've moved in to the village. Christ Rudy what's got in to you these days?"

Rudy said nothing but the fact that he was now being chased across the countryside rankled with him. He followed Joop outside. They may as well drive across to the entrance in to the back lane.

*****

Katrijn picked up the blue telephone on its second ring and listened to the callers message.

She sighed and then spoke. "Things are getting serious. I will have to inform Henrik. He may wish to inform the local force. I will try to persuade him to hold off for a while longer. Take care."

Katrijn replaced the receiver and deliberated over when to tell the Chief Inspector the latest news.

*****

Jason walked up the road to Jake's building. On entering he gave a shout to announce his arrival. It was answered from the mezzanine floor. Jason climbed the stairs to find Jake sat at a computer.

"May have had a stroke of luck." Jason said as he approached Jake. "Make us a coffee and I'll tell you about it."

Jake rose and went across to the coffee machine. "Tell me about it while I get us a drink."

Jason started to explain. "When I opened up this morning, I found an envelope with a note inside. The gist of the message is the name of a woman in Holland who may be able to provide the lead we need to track down Nina's killers. From the poor English and the scruffy writing I would guess it was from one of the Turks. Probably pissed off at the deaths of their mates. How we use this or learn anything from it I don't know, especially as she's in Holland and we're here."

"Yeah. Could be a stumbling block. I'll think about it and make a few enquiries. Do you still want sugar in this?"

They drank their coffee and mulled over the new found information. Jake studied the note and other than come to same conclusion, it was probably from a Turk unknown, could gather no further clues.

Jason returned to his workshop and Jake finished off inputting the data for the previous weeks jobs that had been completed. As soon as that task was finished, he made himself a further cup of coffee and then studied the note Jason had left with him. Sara Meijer. The name of a woman in Holland. No town or where she could be found.

For the rest of the afternoon and deep in to the evening Jake spent his time calling old friends and acquaintances, seeking help. The person he considered the most able to help was unavailable, but his wife said she would get him to call back as soon as he returned from a trip to Germany.

Chapter 39

Colonel Jolyon Carstairs-Smythe, or as Jake knew the man, Captain Joe Smythe. It was in Kosovo that Jake first met the captain.

In 1992 Jake had been in Bosnia. It was here that he experienced the first real love of his life, only for Dzenita to be murdered by an ethnic cleansing force. Her photograph still remained in his wallet and it was now joined by Nina's.

In 1999, the UN passed a Security Council Resolution numbered 1244 to alleviate the grave humanitarian crisis that had developed. There was fighting between forces from Yugoslavia and the Kosovo Liberation Army, with Serb forces carrying out ethnic cleansing atrocities of Kosovo Albanians. At its height there were 50,000 troops deployed from 39 countries, both NATO and non NATO.

Jake, including his sergeant, Dave Brewer, was stationed in the south making regular patrols through two local villages to deter the Kosovo Liberation from making any incursions. There were known to be sympathisers holed up in the village and one was passing information to the intelligence units. However it was thought he had been compromised and he was to be extracted. Jakes normal patrol was joined by an officer, who was able to recognise the man and once they had him back at base, would effect his removal from the area.

The patrol entered the village just before dawn broke. All was silent except for the noises made by the goats and other animals. It took ten minutes before the unknown officer found the house he was looking for. House was rather a stretch of the imagination. In England you would have been found guilty of animal cruelty if you had let wild rats infest the property. Comprising of the one floor with a door at front in the centre, with a window each side of it. Both windows were boarded up. There were no windows down either side and the rear of the building was a mirror image of the front. All appeared to be quiet and there was no sound or movement inside.

I stood with the officer as we approached the door. We stood and listened. Silence. As he was about to tap on the door I heard the distinctive sound of an automatic being cocked. I shoved the officer to one side as I leapt in the opposite direction. There followed the sound of gunshots and splintered holes appeared in the flimsy door just about where we had been standing. I signalled for him to stay down.

"How did you know?" he asked.

"Heard him ready his gun. Silly sod must have put a fresh magazine in and not loaded the first round. Waste of time having the thing if it's not ready to fire."

Dave Brewer came up beside me. "What the fuck was that all about? Daft thing is the noise was enough to wake the dead and yet no one in the village has stirred."

"The villagers will be aware of insurgents and will keep their heads down. Right now, we have to decide what to do about this. We have been fired upon so are perfectly entitled to return fire and defend ourselves. Matey boy here needs to see if his man is still alive and able to be brought out."

Dave put his thumb and index finger together to form a circle mouthed "one minute," then went back the way he had come. A minute later he returned with a couple of grenades. "Stun grenades," he said, "that'll shift the bastards."

The spook officer spoke. "I'd like at least one alive if possible. Would like a quick word with him."

I shrugged my shoulders. My orders were to expedite the escape of the informant and to provide the spook with whatever help he deemed necessary. "Okay, we'll see what we can do."

Dave and I quickly went over our plan of action. The rear of the building was covered by the remaining four of the patrol. Dave the spook and myself would enter through the front door. Dave disappeared again but in a few minutes returned with an axe he had purloined from a neighbours shed. The other officer and I had a grenade ready to throw in to the building, once Dave had wielded the axe and demolished the door.

The almost rotten wood of the door gave way at first stroke of the axe. I threw my grenade in which was quickly followed by the second held by the spook.

All went smoothly with the spook the first to rush in to the building. The shooter was trying to reach the back door but was so dazed; he was staggering along a hallway, bouncing of the walls. There was soft "phut" as the spook shot him in the leg. He cried out and fell to the floor, dropping his weapon, and spreading his arms wide to indicate surrender. There were two further reports of shots fired and a short cry of despair. Must have been at least two I surmised. A search of the rooms showed no more enemy but a woman who had been stripped, lay moaning on the bed, covered in blood. A man, presumably her husband and the man we were to help escape was tied naked to a chair. He had been badly beaten, with numerous cuts to his whole body. His throat had been cut, and blood had sprayed over the bed, his wife, and from a look at our prisoner, his assailant. The spook checked for signs of life. He looked at me and shook his head.

He gave the woman a cursory examination, then turned to me and said softly, "poor cows dying and is probably in extreme pain. She's been raped and assaulted with a knife in both the vagina and anally and from the look of things has also been gut shot." He knelt beside her, "you and your sergeant need to go outside and wait for me. I won't be long."

He began to talk quietly and gently to the woman as I and Dave picked up our weapons and made our way outside. A few minutes later there was that soft "phut" again. A moment later there was scream and I heard the spook converse in what I took to be Serbian. The man screamed again. There was another "phut" and a moment later the spook reappeared.

"We're done here," he said, "Time for us to move on; I have a report to write."

I looked at him and asked, "Is everything kosher in there?"

"The woman is at rest and our Serb friend is, just like the woman was, dying of a gut shot. Hopefully, very painfully." He smiled at me and I grinned back. "Oh! I also need to thank you for saving my life back there. Thank you. It would be better if you called me Joe."

"I'm Jake and there's no thanks necessary, we all cover each others back out here."

Chapter 40

It was two days before I received a return telephone call.

"Jake Beck. Must be nearly twenty years since I heard that name. Must be something important, what can I do for you old boy?"

"Hi Joe. Yeah, it must be twenty years and I have to be honest, I wouldn't have bothered you if it hadn't been important. I need help and I'm not sure where to go."

"Well old chap you tell me the problem and I'll let you know if I can help."

Over the next forty-five minutes Jake told Joe his story. Joe ummed and ahhed, throughout and only interrupted to show sympathy at Nina's death and when he wished a point to be clarified.

A Dish Best Served Cold

"Okay old boy, what is it you are exactly after?"

"I have the name of a woman and am informed that she lives in Holland. I've told you of the two Dutchmen that are being sought by the police in connection with the murder of two Turks, and links to the drug trade. What I don't know is the relationship between them and this woman. I need information on Sara Meijer."

There was silence on the other end of the telephone. "Are you still there Joe?"

"Sorry old boy but I was thinking. Ordinarily I would say I couldn't help, but in your case I owe you………"

Jake interrupted." Joe you owe me nothing and I didn't contact you for a favour but because you're the only person I can think of that may have a solution. Don't compromise yourself on my behalf."

"Whoa1 Whoa1 Whoa! Hold on a mo. I do owe you and I know you are not using that as a lever. As it happens, I have just returned from Germany investigating drugs on one of our few remaining bases. Now if I put her name in to my computer, if there is anything there it will be turned up. If anybody questions my search, I shall say it was a name that I heard while in Germany. Anyway, I'm a full colonel now, so why should anybody query what I do. Bloody hell I run the section."

I laughed. "A full colonel. Congratulations. Seriously, any help you can give will be very much appreciated."

"Think nothing of it. Well must go old boy, I'll be in touch. Toodle pip."

*****

Katrijn knocked on Chief Inspector Henrik Schipp's door and entered on hearing a grunt which from experience was the command to enter.

"You wished to see me sir."

"Ah, Katrijn, yes I need to see you. Take a seat, I won't be a moment." Schipp added some notes to a memo on his desk then sat up and faced Katrijn. "Well my girl what have you done or should I say what has been happening with Operation Doe-Doei (*operation Bye-Bye*). Don't answer that yet but listen to what I have to say. Am I up to date? Why should I be alerted about enquiries being made by British Military Intelligence regarding Sara Meijer? What should I be worried about Katrijn."

"You are au fait with all that has happened. I am still waiting for the next report when I hope to learn where Aken and Van Ess have found to lay low. I think we are very close to having to alert the British authorities of our involvement, if only to protect our agent, especially now they seem to be making enquiries that touch on our operation."

"Thank you Katrijn, I will think this over and make my decision. I will of course discuss with you before informing the British, I may even send you over there to liaise if they agree."

Chapter 41

Sara threw the mobile on to her bed. "Why the fuck would anybody be investigating me?"

Viona picked the phone up and placed it on the bedside cabinet. "Your friend didn't say they were investigating you, he said that they had received enquiries about you. It could mean anything."

"Well it can't be nothing. People aren't looking in to my life because they think I'm going to be the perfect role model for all the saddos that haven't got one. I need to get away, disappear for a while. I need to make some calls." Sara was getting more agitated.

Viona moved over to Sara and gave her hug. "We'll sort it out. Do you want me to come with you? I will, I'll go anywhere for you. I don't understand why you are afraid, and I'm not sure what you are involved in, but I love you Sara and will do anything for you."

"I don't know. I don't even know what I'm going to do, or where I'll go, but yes if it's possible I would like you with me. Now leave me alone, I need to make some arrangements."

*****

Another day, another early morning briefing. Ted glanced around the room to make sure all his team were present. "Thank you for another early start. For some of you it may well be your last, at least for a while. The Super has asked me to scale the team down, at least until we have new information which is likely to lead somewhere. Everything we do these days is governed by costs and he is finding it difficult to justify the expenditure, for so little progress especially when some of you could be more expedient to employ you on cases that can be resolved with a little more manpower. He has promised that if new leads are discovered and progress begins to be made, then the team will be reinforced and you, ladies and gents will be my first choices. I will see each of you in turn today to outline your new tasks. Zoe, you will continue to work with me." This was met with a chorus of 'oooh's and aaah's' before Ted spread his palms downwards and asked them to cool it. "Jonesy you will be covering both camps. Right, that's all for now folks, as I said, I will see each of you during the day, so save any questions for later."

*****

A Dish Best Served Cold

Rudy had sat in an armchair chain smoking and drinking tins of lager. He checked a text on his mobile. "Niels de Groot says Sara and her dyke will be joining us, and we need to lay low for a while. His source in the KLPD says something is afoot but he is out of the loop at the moment. Other than moving to South America or some other shithole, this is as safe as it gets. They don't know about this place. So Joop my old friend, we get lots of beer, fags and some food in and we lie low just like the man said."

"If you say so. I will go out later and get some supplies. The supermarket at Theale stays open until late, so I will wait until dark. Let me know what you want and if you can think of anything Sara and her friend might like.

Rudy lit another cigarette. "I will go to the market. I am going crazy stuck in here. It's worse than being locked up in the slammer. Yeah, and we better open a few windows. Sara will go mad when she finds we've been smoking in here."

"We!" Joop exclaimed. "I don't smoke. She kicks off. You deal with her. I'm going to the fridge for another beer, do you want one?"

Chapter 42

It was three days before Colonel Joe Smythe got back to Jake. "Sorry for the wait old chap, and for leaving it till this late in the day, but my enquiry kicked up a shit storm. Christ knows what you've become involved in, but I've had police agencies, Dutch intelligence, Dutch police and all sorts asking what and why I made the request on Sara Meijer. I'm not even sure what if anything I should pass on to you."

"As I said Joe if it is likely to cause a problem, then forget I asked."

"Glad you said that because what I tell you now did not come from me." Joe drew a breath. "I received quite a dossier on Miss Meijer. She had a troubled upbringing and it was thought she was involved in the death of her father. You may not realise or believe this but you are mentioned in the file."

"Me! How do I manage to be associated with a woman I've never heard of?"

"It was thought that she and her brother killed her father. The reference to you is that the brother was Max Meijer and following his arrest and release in Rotterdam, he was murdered. This was all tied up with the drug gang you had a hand in bringing to justice. She is now thought to be part of the gang supplying drugs in your area. The Dutch police probably know more than they have divulged but I'm hoping there will be more to come in the near future. Well old boy, that's the gist of it. There is one more piece to give you and that is a photo of the woman. It will be in the post. Too risky to e-mail it, too easily traced."

"I don't know how to thank you enough Joe. Needless to say this conversation never took place."

Joe rang off after promising to let me know if anything important was received. I sat back in my chair to mull over what I had just heard. It all went back to Riley. Thinking of Nina, I had tears in my eyes and my heart felt like a solid lump of clay. I laid back and closed my eyes.

It was dark when I awoke. Not late and on the off chance, I punched Jason's number in to my mobile. He answered almost immediately.

"Sorry to ring so late Jason but I've just received some information and I need to tell it to somebody else and decide what to do next. You're more aware of what I am up to than anybody else and I appreciate your views on it all."

Charlie Gardner

*****

Arthur Strong had toiled all day in his allotment. Ever since he had retired six years ago he found enjoyment in the solace of his little shed. Married for over forty two years, both he and his wife found that being together twenty four hours a day was not always bliss. Mabel, his wife, had her own routine and Arthur often found himself in the way.

These days his allotment looked marvellous. The vegetables were the best of all the plots and the flowers were thriving. He would cycle down there in the morning and return at lunchtime. After a bite to eat and a short nap he would return until late afternoon. Before making his way home he would pop in the pub for a pint or two.

Today was Wednesday so his evening meal would be cold cuts and a jacket baked potato, something that never excited his taste buds. The landlord was surprised that Arthur was on his third pint and it was getting dark outside.

"You realise what the time is Arthur? Hope you got lights on that bike of yours. Mabel will start to get worried. You're not usually this late." The landlord, Dave Charlton, had never known Arthur stay this late.

Arthur grunted in acknowledgement then added, "Good as told me to bugger off and live on my allotment this morning, so bugger her, I'll please myself what time I get home." He returned to his pint.

*****

Joop pulled out in to the lane behind the house after checking there was no traffic in either direction. It was almost dark which made it easy to see headlights approaching. He proceeded to the main road through Theale driving carefully. The last thing he needed was to be stopped by the police.

It only took a few minutes to reach the supermarket, grab a trolley, and tour the aisles picking up beer, bread, some frozen meals, a selection of fruit and tins of beans.

He packed the groceries in the Range Rover and made his way back. He carried the bags in to the kitchen and stared to unpack.

"Where are the fags? Don't tell me you've forgotten them you dozy bastard."

Joop started to apologise as Rudy grabbed the keys off the side and slammed the door behind himself as he went outside. Joop heard the powerful V8 roar in to life and gravel being churned up as Rudy tour off.

Chapter 43

Jason listened to Jakes news. Silence followed and for a moment, Jake thought he had been cut off. "Are you still there Jason?"

"Sorry Jake, I'm thinking. Give me ten minutes or so and I will phone you back. Jason rang off.

It was more than thirty minutes before Jake's mobile alerted him to an incoming call.

Jason was apologetic. "Rather longer than I thought, but the more I think about this, the more I think you, or maybe we, ought to go to the police. This may be the intelligence they need to kick-start their investigation"

Jake sounded crestfallen. "I thought you'd say that. When your deliberations began to take so long, I guessed what your answer would be. I can understand why you don't want to get further involved. Maybe we have done all we can and neither of us have the qualifications to act as detectives. I'll sleep on it and make my decision in the morning. Speak tomorrow Jason, and thanks for all you've done."

*****

Despite the beer inside him, Arthur began to have misgivings about his prolonged absence. The bravado of not giving a damn was wearing thin and Arthur was under no illusion that Mabel would give him hell when he finally walked through the door. Decision made he downed the last of his pint, then made his way outside, none to steady on his feet.

He pulled his bicycle away from the railings and wheeled it in to the road. Standing on the left of his machine, he placed his right foot on the pedal and made to mount. His addled brain was still working well enough to let him know that this was never going to work. He looked down to fathom where the problem lay, then giving up, decided he would push the bicycle home. It would take longer but he was in no hurry to be greeted by Mabel.

There was no pavement in the lane and he set off for home. Suddenly he felt the cycle ripped out of his hands and propelled across the grass verge and in to the hedgerow. That was less than a second before Arthur's right leg and hip were struck hard and he was spun round and collapsed on the grass.

At eleven o'clock Mabel phoned the pub only to be told that Arthur had left over half an hour ago. Putting the telephone down, Dave looked down the bar and saw Roy Barber.

"Roy wouldn't do me a favour would you and take a slow ride along the lane and see if Arthur is sat on the verge or passed out. He'd had a few pints when he left here tonight and he was a bit unsteady. Wouldn't like to think anything had happened to the old sod and his missus has just been on the phone a little bit worried. Be worth a drink when you get back and it'll only take ten minutes."

"Daft old bugger is probably sleeping it off in the ditch. Okay, give me a minute to finish this pint and then I'll go. Two pints you said didn't you."

Roy set off, driving slowly along the lane. He had not covered more than a quarter mile before rounding a slight bend in and spotting, in his headlights, Arthur spread out on the verge. Roy pulled over and turned on his hazard warning lights. He stepped out of the car and walked back to where Arthur lay.

"Come on you silly old bugger. Wake up." He muttered. Stepping closer about to bend over and give Arthur a shake, he spotted broken glass. Thinking a little more clearly he realised that even drunk, you would hardly lie in the position that Arthur lay. He knelt down and put his fingers on Arthur's neck, just as he had seen them do on the television. He could not feel a pulse although he was not entirely surprised as he had never had any first aid training or even felt for a pulse before.

He pulled his mobile from his pocket and stared at it for a moment. He had never called the emergency services before and wondered what he should dial. He hit 999 and hoped that would get him connected. There was a delay and Roy thought may be the number was not valid. He was about to end the call when there was a reply.

"I need help. I need an ambulance. An old man has been knocked over. Can you……"

"Calm down sir and give me your name"

Roy took a deep breath and answered the questions directed at him. He was reassured that both the police and paramedics were on there way and he should wait with the injured person until they arrived. Roy finished the call then went to the boot of his car and took out a blanket. It was a little grubby but better than nothing. He covered Arthur then rang Dave back at the pub.

*****

Jake got little sleep. When he did doze off he awoke from the recurring dream of being with Nina. It did not matter what pills he took, or how much whiskey he consumed, his sleep was always disrupted, leaving him depressed.

He rose from the sofa where he had slept after telephoning Jason, and went through to the kitchen to make himself a coffee. Sipping the coffee he considered his options. After a second cup of coffee he understood where his deliberations had led him.

"Right." He thought, "A shower and get dressed then a phone call to make."

Chapter 44

Jake changed his mind about the telephone call and instead drove down in to Reading. Parking up he strode across the road and entered the police station.

He approached the enquiries window and when asked the nature of his enquiry replied, "I'd like to see DCI Potter please. I can wait."

The constable picked up a telephone and after a short conversation told him to take a seat and the DCI would be down in a short while.

Ted took a seat and after a few minutes began to wonder what a 'while' was. What was the difference between a short while and a long while? It did not really matter because while Jake was contemplating this matter the DCI appeared.

A Dish Best Served Cold

"Mister Beck how can I help you?" Ted Potter held his hand out. "I suppose you want to know what progress we've made."

"Actually I don't," answered Jake. "I've come to give you some information that may help."

"I hope you're not going to tell me you have still been investigating your wife's death Mister Beck. I'm not kidding when I say you could be endangering your life. Look what happened when you got involved last time, you damn nearly wound up dead."

"The answer you don't want to here is yes I have, but I am here now to let you know what I have discovered. Can we sit somewhere private?"

Shaking his head, the DCI steered Jake in to an interview room. "Do you mind if I ask my colleague to join us?"

Jake gave his consent and a few moments later DC Zoe Newman was introduced to Jake.

Jake told the whole story from the beginning, starting with the initial enquiries at the Istanbul Grill, right up to the information provided by Joe Smythe, but not disclosing his source.

"If as you say this Sara Meijer is involved and all of this information is kosher, how can I confirm it?"

Jake thought carefully then said, "The information was given to me in strictest confidence and I am unable to give you that name. What I can advise is that you contact the Dutch authorities and ask for her background."

At the mention of the Dutch police Zoe sat up and said, "Where do they come in to this?"

Jake looked at her and replied, "You will have to ask them and then make your own minds up."

Ted promised they would look in to it and then showed Jake out. Returning to the interview room he sat down. "Zoe I want you to get in touch with our colleagues in Holland and find out what you can about this Sara Meijer and ask the question, is there anything to connect her with this Rudy Aken character. If there is something going on and we are not aware of it, I will not be a very happy bunny, and you can tell them that."

Later that afternoon Ted received a telephone call from a Chief Inspector Henrik Schipp.

*****

The investigation in the hit and run incident in Tidmarsh Lane was going nowhere. The officers at the scene had bagged some pieces of glass and there was a scrape of paint on the rear carrier of Arthur's bicycle. Until forensic got back with details regarding the vehicle, the police were relying on the public to provide assistance. So far no one had come forward.

Arthur was on the mend in hospital with a broken hip, a fractured leg and multiple cuts and bruises. Mabel had visited him every day and had given him hell every time for his stupidity.

The police had interviewed Arthur but he could not remember a thing.

Chapter 45

"It is no good Katrijn we cannot keep this operation quiet any longer. I have just been speaking with a Chief Inspector Potter in Reading and he has asked some awkward questions. He has the bare bones of our case and I have told him you will report to him tomorrow morning. I want you either on a late flight tonight or first thing tomorrow morning. Your agents' calls will be diverted to my office in your absence." Henrik Schipp was not a happy man.

"Sir, could I not telephone him. I have a husband to deal with."

"Forget it Inspector. If you wish to remain in covert ops, you will be in Potter's office tomorrow or directing traffic in Amsterdam. This will now be a joint operation with the British."

"But why involve them now. We have infiltrated and monitored their operation and now you wish to include the British Police. Am I to tell them everything? Do they have to know about Joop and Viona? That latest memory stick that Viona delivered has so much information on it. Enough to incarcerate the whole lot of them, and we're only part way through analysing it. There are details of bank accounts, their suppliers in Romania and where the rubbish originates both in Afghanistan and Colombia."

"I don't like to pull rank Katrijn, because this was your operation but I am being ordered by the powers that be to allow the Brits to participate in this operation. They are to be given full access to anything that involves their investigation. It is their country. I have spoken with their Assistant Chief Constable and he is agreeable to you working alongside their DCI. You will run the operation jointly but you are on British soil and if there is disagreement then he will have the final say."

"In other words I have lost control of my own operation."

"It will be what you make of it Katrijn, It is up to you."

"Well in that case I had better get home and pack a bag and placate my husband when he hears of this. What about my Beretta, am I allowed to keep it? You know what the English are like about guns."

"It has been agreed you can carry your weapon. Now get home and pack."

The next morning Katrijn was in Ted Potter's office at eight o'clock. Ted was not there as he was dropping his daughter off at school. Zoe had collected Katrijn from the public area and then brought her upstairs. She introduced herself and DS Andy Jones to Katrijn then sat her in the DCI's office. She also telephoned upstairs and told Superintendent McArthur that the Dutch inspector had arrived. McArthur replied that he was busy and would introduce himself later. Meanwhile she should await DCI Potter. It was a quarter to nine before Ted arrived.

Following welcoming Katrijn to the UK he called Zoe and Andy in to his office. "This is my team. Meet Detective Constable Zoe Newman and Detective Sergeant Andy Jones. There was a larger number and depending on how this develops, I may well have to recall them."

Introductions over, Ted began to outline how the case had progressed. After covering the murders of Nina Beck and the Turks he moved on to the present. "A short while ago we had exhausted our enquiries and lost track of Aken, Smit or whatever else he calls himself, and Van Ess. We believe they have disappeared abroad. The team and investigation were wound down until Jake Beck called to see me and produced details of a connection between Aken, Smit, Meijer and a case he was involved in a couple of years back. That case involved Max Meijer who was later murdered. His death was believed to be part of a tidying up exercise by Eastern Bloc mafia. Beck will not disclose his source and I am not disposed to press him on the matter. Needless to say what he did was create a hoo-hah between your National Police Force and my bosses, which of course is why you're here. In your shoes I would be a little pissed off at losing some of the control of my own operation."

"Well I'll be honest Chief Inspector, if I had my way you would not be involved now. My investigation is far more wide ranging than yours is and involves drug, people smuggling, prostitution and murder, both here and in Holland, Romania, and we suspect, other European countries. I have people who have put their lives on the line to get where we are, so yes, in your words, I am pissed off at having been sidelined by your investigation. However all said I will co-operate although the one provision I make is that I will not endanger my sources or agents. I hope you will agree with that."

"Of course and I would want to protect my people in the same way. Yes, I am a Chief Inspector, but as colleagues, you can call me Ted. I see you as my equal on this. So can we now compare notes and see if any progress can be made." Ted smiled at Katrijn in a conciliatory manner to show he was willing to work alongside her. He was pleased to see her reciprocate.

The DCI suggested that they join DS Jim Calhoun in the Incident room where he had resurrected his whiteboards and the information thereon. With Katrijn's help they cross referenced and linked various scenes and events together. A story began to emerge although there were still pieces of the jig-saw missing. Ted told them all to break for thirty minutes, grab a coffee and check their telephone messages and e-mails.

As the five gathered to continue, Zoe took the DCI to one side. "Guv, since we learnt that Aken was using a Range Rover and from the partial registration that Kevin Hutt provided, I have received details of all vehicles matching that information recorded on cameras in our area. During the break I received a call from traffic of a sighting out on the A340 just outside Pangbourne. Coincidentally it was the same night a cyclist was knocked over and seriously injured and you know me Guv, I don't believe in coincidence."

"Okay, look in to it. There could be something in it." Ted turned back to address the group. "Zoe has just given me a piece of information regarding a possible sighting of a Range Rover. There may or may not be anything in it, we'll have to wait and see."

Jim Calhoun spoke up. "Where was this sir?"

"The A340, just outside Pangbourne. The Tidmarsh Road."

"Sorry but can I be excused for a moment. I need to make a quick phone call." Katrijn interrupted. "It won't take long and could be very important and related to what Zoe has just mentioned."

Ted agreed and asked the others if they had anything else to say. No one did so he told them to get about their business.

Chapter 46

"Keep a low profile I said. Don't attract attention. But no, you two crazy bastards couldn't do that. I arrive to find the Range Rover with a damaged wing and a police incident board asking for help a few hundred yards from here. You Rudy are becoming a fucking liability. All I asked you to do was come to England, hurt Beck, and set up the drug supplies. Beck's investigation was on the back burner, but you, you had to go and kill two fucking Turks and start a shit storm."

Rudy tried to speak but Sara continued. "I am even being investigated in Holland because of noises the Brits are making over there. Enquiries from all bloody angles, because you can't leave well enough alone. How many times have I told you, I provide the brains, you just do as instructed."

Rudy jumped to his feet absolutely seething. "I'm not your fucking lackey Sara. Me and Max we got on just fine. He trusted me and I trusted him. Don't start ordering me about like a fucking servant. I think a lot of you but I won't be treated like shit, by you or anyone else." He turned and left the room, slamming the door behind him.

Sara called after him. "If you can't handle orders say so and Joop can take over. And don't fucking smoke in my house. And if you and Joop are so close you don't want to step on each others toes then Cuza's man Van Winkel is still over here and he can take charge. And one other thing Rudy, that is the last time you walk out on me, do you hear me you bastard."

Viona had listened to the row, which could be heard all over the house, from the bedroom upstairs. It was now nearly midnight and Sara had been put in a foul mood the moment she arrived and could smell smoke in the house. When she spotted the Range Rover parked out the back she went wild. She would report in at the earliest opportunity. Sara came in to the room and Viona could see the rage within her. She realised she would suffer tonight as Sara always needed to hurt somebody when she was in this mood.

Early in the morning Sara's mobile rang. The screen indicated it was Niels de Groot. They spoke for a few moments before Sara ended the call then threw the mobile across the room smashing a dressing table mirror.

*****

A Dish Best Served Cold

It was an early start for the team. Katrijn had contacted Ted at six thirty that morning with news that both delighted and bothered him.

Ted called the team together and explained what had occurred and that a plan was being put together to raid a property in Tidmarsh. Because firearms were involved it would be under the direction of the firearms unit, Whilst he had the team together he asked that they remain tight lipped about the planned raid. It was not known if the gang were aware that the police knew of their whereabouts. He did not believe any of them were involved but a leak had let the suspects know that the information had originated through Beck.

A helicopter pass had been made and there were two vehicles, one a black Range Rover and the other a blue Mazda MX5, were at the property. The fly pass could not be made at a low enough altitude to recognise the number plates.

Whilst the team waited in the incident room, Ted and Katrijn went to his office to discuss how the matter would be dealt with if arrests were made.

*****

Following the call from De Groot, Sara had searched and found Rudy, having a smoke in one of the outbuildings. "You have thirty minutes to pack a bag and get out of here."

"You're throwing me out?" Rudy was incredulous.

"No I'm saving your miserable skin. The police are on to us and are preparing to raid the place. I took a drive out and every road is covered. You and Joop need to cut across the fields keeping to the trees or hedgerows. Find somewhere you can lay up for a few days while I work on a plan to get you out of the country. Don't contact me. If you need to get in touch phone De Groot. Are you okay for cash?" Rudy nodded. "This has all come about because that bastard Beck has stuck his nose in our business again. It was a mistake letting him live. He should have died along with that whore of a wife of his." Her vitriolic would have carried on if her mobile had not alerted her to an incoming call. It was De Groot. It was just to reiterate his warning and to tell Sara how to play her part. They had no hard evidence against her and all she had to do was deny all knowledge of Rudy's wrongdoings and play dumb with regard to the drug dealing.

They returned to the house where Rudy and Joop gathered essential belongings together then leaving by the back door made good their escape.

Viona realised there was something amiss when Sara returned from outdoors with Rudy. The men disappeared upstairs and within a few minutes were out the door and gone. Sara explained what had happened and told her they were going upstairs to bed as the police would be arriving soon and they needed to act all innocent, or as Sara said not that innocent. With the men gone, they might as well enjoy having the house to themselves.

It was over an hour before the police made their presence known.

Chapter 47

Superintendent McArthur looked at Ted, Katrijn, and then at the newcomer, Inspector James Robertson. "Is everybody in place?" Both men and Katrijn confirmed they were ready to go. "Okay," said McArthur, "Then you're in charge Inspector. Tell your men to take care but not to risk their lives. We know this man is armed and has killed before."

Inspector Robertson replied, "They're good officers, well trained and will not shoot unless there is a risk to life. I know I'm repeating myself but nobody is to enter those premises until I give the all clear. Right let's get this show on the road."

Ted and Superintendent McArthur sat patiently in the communications van listening to Inspector Robertson directing his troops. Covert entry had been made over the front gate and through the rear of the property. There had been a variety of weapons on display from Glock 17 pistols to Heckler and Koch MP5's. Two officers were stationed front and rear, at a vantage point, with Heckler and Koch G3 sniper rifles.

The door was knocked loudly and the instruction to open up was shouted, quickly followed by the door being smashed open. A lot of noise was heard and movement from various head cams seen as the officers moved from room to room. There was a moment of laughter and an officer heard to say, "Thanks for the show ladies and I'd love to watch some more, but you need to put your hands where I can see them and slowly get out of the bed and lay face down on the floor." The officer called for female back up and Robertson ordered a female officer to attend the apprehension of Sara and Viona.

It was a while before all the rooms were declared safe and Ted and Katrijn were able to enter the house. Sara and Viona had been allowed to get dressed, but there was no sign of Rudy or Joop. Despite their protestations, the women were led out to a police car and whisked away to the station for questioning.

"Where are they then?" McArthur looked at Ted as if to hold him responsible that their chief suspects could not be found.

"I'm damned if I know. One thing is for sure, when I find out who has leaked information they'll wish that hanging was an alternative to what I have in store for them."

"Whatever, this is not as though it was a leak to the newspapers; this operation has been revealed to an interested party in Holland. I want to see you in my office as soon as we are back at the station." McArthur turned on his heels and walked away to his waiting car and driver.

"Bollocks that's all I bloody need," thought Ted. "An investigation, within, another investigation."

He walked away to find Katrijn. She was talking to Andy Jones who was overlooking a search of the property It was nearly an hour since the beginning of the raid and for house that was mainly unoccupied, a thorough search was going to take the rest of the day. From a room believed to have been slept in by either Aken or Van Ess, a dog was given a pillowcase to gain a scent. It was then led around the perimeter of the surrounding land where it picked up a trail across the fields. After a couple of miles, the dog handler came across cottage where the trail went cold. The property looked unoccupied and he radioed for assistance before entering.

Robertson and four officers arrived and effected entry through an unlocked door to find an old couple bound and gagged in their bedroom. They were lying on the bed. The man was unconscious with a bloody wound to the left side of his head. The woman lay alongside him whimpering. An ambulance was called and the couple set free. She said the men had burst in, and demanded the keys to the car. When her husband refused they knocked him about a bit but he still would not give up his car keys. Finally they hit her husband on the head and he lost consciousness.

They then forced her to give them the car keys. In tears, she said although they hit her husband the older man said not to hit the woman and he would persuade her to find the keys. She thought that the older man called the other one Rudy.

After tying them up, they left in the car more than two hours ago. She did not know the make of the car or the registration, her husband looked after all of that, and in any case she did not drive. She did remember the logbook and insurance was in the sideboard drawer. Finding the logbook one of the officers radioed through the details.

The ambulance and a female officer arrived and Robertson told her to accompany the old couple to the hospital and to inform DCI Potter immediately if either of them remembered anything significant. Knowing that the suspects were no longer in the area he the DI stood his men down and told them to return to the Lower Earley station get some rest and food and await further orders.

*****

"Where are we going Rudy?"

"Somewhere that will do us for one night until we can sort ourselves out."

Rudy continued driving towards Reading. He knew it was a risk but reckoned it would be a good hour before the police found the old man and the old lady. He had not wanted to hit the old man but he was a stubborn old sod and he did not argue with Joop when he told him to leave the old woman alone. Reading was big enough for them to get lost in, at least for a couple of days.

A Dish Best Served Cold

*****

Back at Reading Ted knocked on McArthur's and hearing a grunt, entered. "You wished to see me sir."

"Come in and take seat." McArthur fiddled with a few bits of paper on his desk then spoke. "Right pigs ear that turned out to be. No arrests other than that woman and her friend. From what I saw of them on the TV link that must have been a chargeable offence. When are you going to interview them?"

"I'll debrief the squad first. They can sit in a cell and stew for a while. Before that, I have something to discuss with you. It concerns Inspector Spronk."

"Stop there Ted. The reason I wished to see you was for the same reason. Two leaks in as many days. Just the same amount of time that Inspector Spronk has been with us. What are your thoughts?"

"I'm in a quandary over this. I would stake my life on it not being one of my own team but having talked with Katrijn I cannot believe it is her. Maybe it's vanity but I pride myself on knowing when someone is not telling me the truth. We spoke at length and she is as committed to the apprehension of Aken and Van Ess as we all are. The problem I have, is what if I am wrong. Any chance you could speak to your opposite half in Holland and gain a little more background information?"

"I concur with you, and yes I will phone her superior officer in Holland and let you know what I learn. I assume you heard about the old couple and the stolen car. It has only just come over the radio so your team may not have brought you up to speed yet. Maybe with a little luck we find the bastards after all. Anyway I'll not waste any more of your time, I'll let you get on."

As Ted was rising from the chair he answered, "Yeah, I heard about the car. Fingers crossed."

Chapter 48

Rudy parked in the Tesco car park then walked through the rows of cars, past the store entrance and out in to the Oxford Road. Crossing the road they made their way to the Istanbul Grill. They did not enter the restaurant but made their way round the back. Not bothering to knock they pushed open Ishak's office door and strode straight in.

"Hello Ishak my old friend. Pleased to see me?"

"It would be dishonest of me to say yes. Many of my friends and the people who live here would like to see you dead. Mehmet and Yunas may not be good boys but they had many friends. It is not safe for you here. I cannot guarantee your safety. You should go." Ishak had a worried look on his face.

Rudy raised his right hand and tapped just under his left armpit. "I have all the protection I need right here. What I don't have is somewhere to lay my head for a day, maybe two."

"But I have nowhere for you to stay. What's up with a hotel? Why do you think I can help?"

Because you have this place. What's upstairs?"

"Some old rooms that are not used. They can't be used because the floorboards are rotten and unsafe. I can't let you sleep up there you may injure yourselves."

"Well, I'll be the judge of that. Now is it through that door? Come on Joop lets inspect our bedroom."

Rudy and Joop followed by Ishak went through the door with Ishak stressing they should take care, as the stairs were not all they should be.

The first room they looked in had a broken window and a hole in the ceiling about two feet square. A pair of pigeons disappeared through the gap and presumably through a further hole in the roof. The floor was covered in droppings and feathers.

"This must be your room," quipped Rudy.

They moved on and inspected three other rooms. In two, the floors were just as Ishak described them, rotten. The third was at least dry and with a quick clean with a broom, would do for a night or two. Rudy told Ishak to send someone for a couple of sleeping bags and either camping mattresses or camp beds.

*****

Sara was interrogated by Ted and Zoe. She maintained her innocence and stated, that as the owner of the property in Tidmarsh, she was entitled to stay there as and when she pleased. When she arrived, she found Rudy Aken and a friend of his living there. She had not given them permission to stay there and asked them both to leave. Aken had been a friend of her brother and may have known of the property through him.

"That is all I am saying Chief Inspector so either charge me or let me go. Up to you, but my next action will be to phone my solicitor who I have no doubt will have me released in a very short time." Sara gave Ted and Zoe a large smile.

Ted beckoned to the constable also present, and told him to put her back in the cells.

"You can't do that you bastard. You've nothing to charge me with."

"You can wait until after I have questioned your girlfriend." Ted rose and left the room along with Zoe.

Back in his office, Ted admitted to Zoe that they were going to have to let Sara Meijer go, as they had nothing to hold her on. Before that, he and Inspector Spronk were going to interview the Dutch girlfriend.

Viona listened as Katrijn explained the agreement that she had reached with the British police regarding her and Sara.

"Without exposing you, we have no evidence here in the UK that Sara was complicit in the murders that Aken has committed. Unless Aken implicates her in the murders then she may never be charged with conspiracy to murder. From what you have already given us, Viona, then the import and supply of drugs is a given. By letting you and Sara walk out of here with no charges against, should strengthen your position. It is hoped that in the not to distant future we will then have plenty of evidence against her supplier and the drug pushers both here in the UK and across the rest of Europe. How are you? You look relaxed enough but I know this cannot be easy for you."

"I'm coping well. I had no idea when I took this on, what it would be like making love to a woman. If I were a man, I'd say I've risen to the occasion." Viona gave a little chuckle. "Actually, it's not too hard. She is easy to get on with if you make allowances for her selfishness. There is just one thing I should tell you. When Sara and Rudy were talking in the stable, I could overhear them upstairs in the bedroom with the window open. She wants Beck dead."

"Okay, I take that onboard, but at the first sign of trouble you get out and I'll arrange for you to be picked up. I mean that Viona, first inkling of a problem and you make your escape." Katrijn looked at Ted. "Is there anything you wish to say or add?"

A Dish Best Served Cold

Ted looked at Viona. "I know Viona is not your proper name but I would say that whoever you are, you are a very brave lady."

Viona smiled. "I have my own personal reasons for wanting these people behind bars."

Ted began to rise from his chair. "We'll have you returned to your cell for an hour or so then you'll both be set free."

Chapter 49

"No trace of the car and not a word on the street about them. Where the hell are they? What am I missing? They can't just vanish in to thin air." Ted was walking back and forth in the incident room.

"Guv we have every snout on the street looking for information to claim the reward on this one, but not a word." DS Andy Jones looked at the rest of the team. "Anybody got an idea, anything?" Nobody spoke.

"Can't we wait until he makes a move on Beck?" It was Zoe's voice from across the room.

"We could but who's to say that they will attempt to kill Beck. They might just decide to make a run for the Continent. No, we need to be proactive on the street. Put pressure on your snouts. Somebody must know where they're hiding." Ted's gaze swept around the room. "Beck has an armed officer in the house with him. Additionally there are surveillance teams in the area. Right ladies and gents, let's get to it. Zoe can you pop in to my office, and do me a favour and bring me a coffee please." Ted left the team to get on with it.

Andy looked at Zoe. "Bet he never pays you for the coffees."

Ted was waiting for Zoe to return with his coffee when Andy knocked on the door and poked his head in. "Cars been found guv, Tesco car park off the Oxford Road. I'm just off to see if there's anything to be learnt."

"Doubt that Andy but have a look around and let me know. I'm popping out to Riseley to check on arrangements out there and see if Beck knows anything else that may help us."

Ted drove out to Becks property on the old Basingstoke Road. There was a pub at the junction with Part Lane and in the car park he spotted an unmarked car which he recognised as one of their own. He drove down the lane past the few large properties until he reached Beck's. Slowing down he looked up the driveway. The only vehicle was a Jeep that he knew was Beck's and was pleased to see that no other cars showed. Carrying on there was a further property with a small Vauxhall van belonging to a builder together with a board stood outside to display that the extension was being carried out by Moran's a local contractor. Further down the lane a car was parked on the verge. Right, thought Ted, everything appears to be in place. Other than approaching over the fields or by helicopter, there was no other means of gaining access to the property.

Returning to the house, Ted knocked on the door. He heard a bolt being withdrawn and the door opened to show Beck stood there in his pyjamas.

Ted stared for a moment then spoke. "Good afternoon Mister Beck, may I come in?"

Jake mumbled his consent and Ted entered and followed Jake through to the kitchen. Sitting and watching a monitor, split in to four screens was sergeant Tony Bishop, who was usually to be found in an Armed Response Vehicle, but who had been purloined by Ted for this job.

"Hi Tony, everything okay?" Ted took a seat at the table.

"Quiet, very quiet. What brings you out here sir? Hoping to catch me asleep I bet."

"No Tony, I especially requested you for this job. I needed experience and a level head. Sorry if it's buggered up your cushy life of riding around in a car all day."

Tony laughed, "I wish."

Jake took a cup of tea the side and made for the stairs. "I'll be up in my bedroom if you want me."

"Is he alright?" Ted enquired.

"Doctor came round earlier. He's depressed. To begin with he was euphoric that we now had somebody in our sights, but that rapidly changed to how you see him now.

Gave him some pills but said they might take a while to kick in. Spends most of his time in his bedroom. I make him drinks and try to talk, but he's a little reticent to chat much. Problem is I need to be here monitoring these screens."

Ted rose from the table. "Just going to have a quick look around. Seen it before, but I just wish to refresh my memory."

Ted tapped on the bedroom door and without waiting for an answer stepped in to the room. Jake lay on the bed but sat up and twisted to sit on the side of the bed facing Ted. Jake looked up. "Sorry but not the best of company at the moment."

Ted put his hand on Jake's shoulder. "You have my sympathy mister Beck, it's been a long and arduous journey and I can't even promise that it's over yet."

"For me this will never be over. I relive Nina's murder every day. If I could get hold of this bastard Aken before you, I'd kill him and bugger the consequences. Do you know that even that would never get rid of the pain I feel."

"I cannot begin to imagine the hurt you feel, but believe me I will nail this bastard. Leave the apprehending and punishment of Aken to us and the courts. Last job I require is arresting you. We'll talk again." Ted turned and left the room

Jake swallowed a couple of the pills and lay back on the bed.

Chapter 50

Ted was just climbing in to his car when his mobile rang. The screen showed it was DS Andy Jones. "Hi Andy, what's up?"

"Wanted to let you know, CCTV shows Aken and Van Ess crossing the Oxford Road and walking west. We then lose them because of a malfunctioning camera."

Ted interrupted. "And that's good news?"

"Yeah, because on the next camera they don't appear, and what is between these two cameras, the Istanbul Grill. Now that place is mentioned in Inspector Spronk's report. Bad news is we have been told to steer clear so as not to jeopardise their investigation. Need your advice on this but in the meanwhile I have DC Collins watching the place."

"Well done Andy, I should be back in half an hour."

When got back the room was buzzing. Inspector Spronk was on her mobile. Ted beckoned her to follow him through to his office. Sitting at his desk he telephoned McArthur and discussed his plan, then waited for Inspector Spronk to join him.

A few minutes later she stepped in to the office and Ted indicated she should sit down.

"No doubt you're aware we have a lead on Aken and Van Ess. Problem is we believe they're holed up in one of your targets. These people are killers and I'm of the opinion that murder trumps your drug dealing charge." Katrijn made a move to say something. "Hear me out. I have a plan which I think will work. It's been discussed with the Super and he agrees with me, with the provision that you're kept in the loop. Here's what I suggest."

Because of the danger of firearms being involved, Ted placed an ARV at each end of the street. The search team from the Firearms Unit were sitting in a Transit van just around the corner. Ted gave the nod to Inspector Robinson and there was the clatter of running feet as the unit ran in to the alley and after shouting their warning walked in through an unlocked door.

Ishak and Kaya were in the office and looked petrified as a sergeant yelled, "Get down on the floor. Where are Aken and Van Ess?"

Two other officers had already started to climb the stairs. There were shouts, doors being forced open and further shouts of clear. The same was occurring in the restaurant and take-away. An almighty crash almost had a young constable discharge his weapon at an unexpected intrusion. His weapon had not been on safety and his finger was inside the trigger guard. Luckily the bullet was embedded in a sideboard full of dinner and side plates, mainly broken dinner and side plates. The young officer was cursing as he realised there would be hell to pay for his mistake.

Entering a room above the rotten floor gave way and the unfortunate individual plunged through the ceiling, landing on a table loaded with glass and crockery.

Given the all clear, McArthur gave permission to enter the premises. Ishak and Kaya were uncuffed and allowed to stand.

Giving Ishak a hard look DS Andy Jones demanded, "Where are the Dutchmen? They were seen coming here." Not quite true but police are allowed a little leeway when questioning people. "You can be done for harbouring a criminal. Do you want to be banged up?"

Before he could answer DC Andrea Thorowgood entered from the stairway. "Somebody, and probably Aken, has been sleeping rough upstairs. There's fag ends all over the place and DNA will pinpoint who it was."

Okay. Okay they were here, but only for one night. They couldn't stand the rats. They left yesterday morning. I don't know where they were going. I only let them stay because they threatened my family. What was I to do? Those men are murderers."

"Alright, you and your hoppo here give us descriptions of what they were wearing, and we may reconsider any charges. If they left yesterday morning, why haven't you informed us? Think on, your not in the clear yet." The DS made towards the door.

"Hey, what about the damage to my restaurant? Who is going to pay for fixing that?"

"See the DC." Andy left the DC to get on taking descriptions of the men.

Back at the station Ted sat in his office going through the interview notes of Sara Meijer and Viona when Superintendent McArthur appeared in the doorway.

Not entering but leaning on the door frame he remarked, "It's bloody exasperating Ted but we always seem to be two paces behind these Dutch killers. Did you get to the bottom of our leak? Is someone passing on information?"

"No I didn't but I am certain it was nobody on my team. I would vouch for any one of them. If I'm proved wrong you can take me in the car park, stand me against the wall and shoot me. Better still I'll do it myself. As far as I am aware no further leaks have occurred. I am keeping an eye on the situation and if necessary will instigate an inquiry."

McArthur pursed his lips and slowly nodded his head up and down.

Chapter 51

What Ishak Onder had not told the police was that Aken and Van Ess had taken his old and battered Renault van. Aken was of view that the police would not be expecting them to be in such a rubbish vehicle.

Leaving Reading on the A33 Basingstoke Road Joop asked, "Where are we going, back to Aldershot?"

Rudy raised his eyebrows. "Don't be stupid, the police already know of that place. I'm going where the black bitch lived, only this time I'll finish off the husband. That arsehole Beck has interfered in my life for the last time."

"But risky isn't it. The *smeris* are sure to have men in place to provide protection. They're not just going to sit back and let you get anywhere near the place."

"Joop my old buddy, I did not spend six years with the *Korps Commandotroepen* for nothing. Outwitting a few dumb British pigs will be child's play. All I want you to do is watch my back."

"I hope you're right. Don't you think you're getting a little old to be playing soldiers?"

"Whatever you may think, I am not playing."

Just after the junction with the M4 Rudy told Joop to take the old road through the villages of Three Mile Cross and Spencers Wood. As they approached The Mill House at Swallowfield, Rudy told Joop to take the next left. Following the road, they came to a junction.

"Go straight over, then an almost immediate right. I don't want to go through the village."

Driving on Rudy told Joop to take a left. "This road takes us back to the other side of the village. We'll pull up just over here on the left in that gateway and I'll show you where Beck's house is. Looking across the fields Rudy pointed out the few properties in the distance, over on the right."

"Turn the van around here and then we'll do a drive past, not to fast, not to slow. I think its time to set this little toy in motion."

On the way out of Reading Rudy had purchased an in vehicle journey recorder. Not much bigger than his fist, the device was affixed to the windscreen by means of a suction cup. Powered from the cigarette lighter socket it would record for hours. Whilst Joop drove, Rudy made a mental note of all the properties and vehicles he saw en route. A lot of it he remembered from the reconnoitring of the surrounding area over twelve months ago. Not a lot had changed.

"Right Joop, when we hit the main road follow it through to Basingstoke and we'll find us a small B and B for the next night or so. We'll also dump this van and hire a car."

*****

Maybe the pills were beginning to kick in but Jake felt a lot better when he awoke in the morning. He joined Tony Bishop in the kitchen and even offered to cook breakfast.

Chatting over a plateful of scrambled eggs on toast, Jake was surprised how much Tony knew about him. "I've read the file we have on you," declared Tony. "I'm surprised you didn't join the force. Your detective work nailing the Riley family was brilliant even if it nearly got you killed, not once but twice."

"It wasn't twice it was damned near three times. It's how I met Nina. I'm unlucky for women. The two I've loved have both been murdered." Realising what he had just said, Jake felt a sadness and gloom descend upon him. "I'll just pop upstairs if you'll excuse me Tony, got a few things to sort out."

With Jake back in his room, Tony placed the pan, plates, cups and cutlery in the dishwasher. "Poor bastard," he thought. "Didn't even know he'd another wife or whatever she was murdered. There was no mention of it in the file." Finished tidying away he took a stroll outside to both exercise after the breakfast and inspect the house and surrounding area.

As Jake entered his bedroom, he could feel the tears gathering in his eyes. "Fuck! Fuck! Fuck!" he murmured to himself, beginning to lose control of his emotions. He lay on the bed for a while, gathering his thoughts and fighting the urge to go to sleep and forget.

Mentally pulling his thoughts and himself together, he went back downstairs to the kitchen. Tony was not there. He unlocked the connecting door to the garage. Nina's car still there gathering dust took him aback momentarily as it did every time he used he used his mini gym. At the far end of the garage was a rowing machine, multi gym, treadmill and weights. They had been Nina's present to him.

His regime was not strict but he liked to work out when he had time to spare. After a few stretches and limbering up exercises, he moved over to the treadmill. The MP3 player was hanging there as usual and he popped in the earpieces and switched it on. Turning on the treadmill, he began a gentle jog. Listening to the music and gently exercising he entered another world.

Chapter 52

"Tonight Joop we are going to do a dummy run. I know we've been there before, but last time we walked in through the front door. I need to check that I can get in through the back without being seen. There is sure to be a copper in the house with him and I need to see where he spends his time and if there's more than one. I've seen the two cars covering the roads that give access to the property, but I will need to see if there is any cover for the rear of the house. All I need you to do is drop me at that farm gate and then drive down to The Wellington Arms where we'll take a couple of rooms for a few days. You okay with that?"

"Yeah, I've no problem with that, but what if you get seen, I shall be a few miles away."

"I will make my way through the fields and trees. I am more than capable of avoiding capture. Once I feel safe,

I will phone you and you can come and pick me up. That isn't going to happen Joop; I will recce my plan of attack tonight and then decide when to put it in action. Meanwhile we'll get to bed and be ready to leave here at 03.00 hours."

Whilst staying in Basingstoke, Rudy had been shopping at an army surplus store. He'd purchased a pair of cammo pants and top plus a pair of soft leather boots. He'd spent the last two days walking around in the boots to work the leather and ensure they were a comfortable fit.

Joop hid a laugh but couldn't help grinning at Rudy as he appeared. "Fucking hell, you look as if you are off to war."

Rudy scowled. "Mock all you like but I do not intend to get caught. If they spot me then I will have no further chance to nail the bastard." He picked up his pistol from the table and inspected the magazine to make sure it was fully loaded. He knew it would be but it was second nature to check. He was getting back in to the role of his Special Forces days. "I'm ready let's go." He left the room at the B and B carrying what other belongings he had. They would not be returning. Rudy placed an envelope in the kitchen, so that Joan who owned the B and B would spot it when she rose at five thirty to begin her day. There was enough to cover their bill and five pounds extra, with a post it note saying thank you. Rudy had thought of leaving without paying but wished to avoid any chance of Joan informing the police.

It took only twenty-five minutes to reach the farm gate. Joop dropped Rudy off and drove away without waiting. Rudy had blacked his face during the journey and now pulled on a pair of soft leather gloves. There was only a quarter moon but when there was no cloud covering it, there was adequate light to illuminate Rudy's way. He climbed silently over the gate and then hugging the hedgerow made his way round the edge of the field towards Jake's property. It would have been quicker to cut straight across the field, but the risk of being seen if there was a spotter in an upstairs room would have been greater. He just hoped they did not have heat-seeking gear.

He ran at a crouch until he was a hundred metres from the rear of Beck's land. Dropping flat he belly crawled to the boundary of hedge that separated pasture from manicured lawn. The house lay about fifty metres away, with a lawn interspersed with flower beds, a small vegetable plot and an area enclosed by panelling hiding an oil tank. There was a light showing through an upstairs window, possibly a hall light. There was also a glimmer of a light shining through a door. He lay absolutely still listening for over five minutes for any sound that should not be there. He moved slowly along the hedge looking an access point. The hedge was about five feet tall and any attempt to go over it would be noticeable in daylight. At the foot, he discovered a broader gap between the base of the bushes. By rolling on to one side, he should just be able to squeeze through. His clothes were slick with the dew and he worried that crawling over the grass would leave a tell tale trail.

Once through he was careful to tread as close to the hedgerow as possible until he came to the vegetable patch. From there he was able to travel a hogging path that led to some concrete hard standing at the rear of the garage. He stopped and listened. Nothing. Keeping low, he made his way along the wall to the first window. Raising is head just enough to see inside he was able to make out from the glow of the downstairs light that he was looking in to the kitchen. Stealthily moving to his right he came to the back door that led straight in to the kitchen. On the far side of the room another door was ajar, and from what he could see, led through to the hallway. Moving on were patio doors. Not a lot of light and as he was about to move to the corner of the building, a slight movement caused him to freeze. Somebody was sitting in an armchair looking directly down the garden. Rudy stopped and watched the person for a few minutes. The unknown man rose from the chair walked to the patio doors and stared out. After a few seconds, he turned and walked away and a moment later, the kitchen light came on. Rudy turned and crept to the back door. The man was making himself a hot drink.

The kitchen light went out and the man returned to his armchair. Rudy had learnt all he needed to know and made his way back the farm gate where he called Joop to collect him.

Chapter 53

Tony Bishop called in next morning as agreed. "Not sure, but had a feeling last night that there was somebody sneaking around last night. Cliff was on watch and he said he saw nothing out of the ordinary. You do get animals in the garden both day and night. I'll take a stroll around the perimeter after this call and see if I can spot anything. I'll let you know if I find anything."

Tony swallowed the last of his tea and toast. Grabbing his jacket and checking his Glock he shouted to Jake who was upstairs that he was going for a wander around the garden.

Stepping out of the front porch, he crossed the gravel drive to the front gate. His footsteps were noisy enough in the day, in the quiet of the night they would be even worse. There was no silent way to approach the front of the house, only by using the drive, or coming through the hedge and across the grass. The grass was still wet with dew with nothing to show it been disturbed in the night. Taking slow steps, Tony carefully inspected the edge of the lawn as he went. When he came to the gap Rudy had slipped through, he bent down and looked more closely. After a minute or two he moved on until he was back at the front door. He then proceeded to follow the edge of the brickwork, before returning to the kitchen. Cliff was sound asleep in the guest room so Tony thought he would leave asking him to look at the gap in the hedge until later.

Reporting to DCI Potter, he mentioned what he had seen, but as the gap was an animal run he would ask DS Cliff Morgan to have a look when he awoke. The DCI confirmed that the DC's in the unmarked cars could not recount any unusual activity or vehicles during the night. The only vehicles had belonged to locals.

It was four in the afternoon before Cliff roused himself and joined Tony in the sitting room. "Been quiet Tony?"

"Nothing happening today but I would like you to look at a gap in the hedge I've found. Probably nothing but a second pair of eyes if you know what I mean."

"Sure, where's Jake?"

"In his den, buggering about on his computer. He had a coffee with me earlier and was quite chatty. Talked a little of his family and his service days. Also spent some time in his little gym, which by the way he says we are free to use. Might have a go later."

"You need too! I'll go and see if he wants a coffee."

Cliff returned a minute later. "Says he'll join us for a coffee in five minutes."

Jake Cliff and Tony sat around the kitchen table drinking coffee and eating biscuits. Taking on a serious tone, Tony looked at Jake. "God forbid but if Aken and Van Ess should make an attempt to enter the house, I need to be certain you know what to do. You make straight for the bedroom at the top of the stairs and lock yourself in. Pull the cabinet across in front of the door and use the spare mobile up there to call 999."

"I know! I know!. Don't worry I know what to do."

"Jake, this isn't a game. Aken is a killer. I know we're relaxed at the moment and not one of us is wearing our bullet proof vest as we should be, but mine is here on the chair as is Cliff's. Do you even know where yours is?"

Jake looked blank. "In my bedroom I think."

"Wrong place. If you had to rush upstairs now it would be in the wrong place. Wear it or at least carry it with you from room to room. I don't need you injured or worse 'cos you can't even carry out the simple things. Jake you've probably, no, definitely, been fired upon more than I ever will be, so please for my peace of mind take this threat seriously."

"I am Tony. Maybe my mind isn't in the right place. I don't know. Why the sudden lesson?"

A Dish Best Served Cold

Before Tony could answer his mobile rang. There was a short conversation with Tony nodding and acknowledging what was said.

Tony turned his attention back to Jake. "I'm reiterating everything because there is a chance somebody was out in the garden last night. It may have been an animal but best to be careful. With what I have just learnt there is even more reason to be cautious. Aken was a member of the Dutch Special Forces. I was also told that you have a shotgun licence. Where do keep your guns?"

"Gun cabinet is in my den, walnut case and leaded door. The steel panel behind it looks like rows of books."

"I need the keys Jake. Sorry but the last thing Cliff and I need is for you to be lose with a shotgun if the shit hits fan."

"I have spent more time with guns and rifles than you have Tony and I am quite safe with a gun in my hand. There's no reason for you to have my keys."

"Sorry Jake but that's the way it has to be. I don't want to argue over this."

Jake shrugged his shoulders and went through to the utility room, followed by Tony. Going to a wall cupboard he opened the door, removed a box of soap powder, giving himself access to a small safe. Jake punched in the combination and opened the door. He sifted through some bits and pieces and withdrew his hand, holding a bunch of keys in his fingers. He turned and threw them to Tony.

"Do you mind if I look? I'm not checking, I'm just interested in what's there. What make is it?"

"Take a look, there's a nice Browning. I can't stop you anyway. If you read the licence it says the police are free to inspect the guns and cabinet anytime they want."

"I'm not inspecting, I'm just interested."

Jake walked back through the kitchen and upstairs to his bedroom. He entered and lay on the bed. Tony may know he had a gun licence but he didn't know there were two guns listed on it. The Browning over and under, and a Remington Auto, both twelve bore.

The Remington was under his bed loaded with three seven-ounce cartridges. Originally the auto would have taken five cartridges but a change in the law meant you had to have the magazine crimped so only a maximum of three could be loaded.

Chapter 54

Rudy had Joop drop him off at the farm gate, telling Joop he would call him when he needed picking up. Climbing over the gate and hugging the hedge, he repeated his journey to the rear of Jake's garden. Three thirty in the morning, just about the time the watcher would start to feel tired. Extracting a mobile phone from his pocket, he fixed it to a branch in the hedge. He knocked it and it fell three inches turning the screen so that it faced the field. On the field side of the hedge, he hung a flak jacket.

Rudy made his way to the patio doors in order to spy on the man sitting in his armchair. Be patient he said to himself. The man yawned, fidgeted and the settled back against the cushions.

Rudy waited. The man sat up and yawned again. This time he placed his hands on the arms of the chair to help himself rise. Rudy hit the send on his mobile and in the still of the night heard the mobile in the hedge vibrate and saw the screen light up before it dulled a little as it turned.

The man had seen it too, and stepped close to the glass door and placing his hand against the glass and above his eyebrows stared at the point in the hedgerow where the light had dulled and then extinguished.

Rudy watched him carefully. The man rubbed his eyes then took another look. Come on thought Rudy you know you want to know what it was. The next move was crucial. Would he wake his partner or, human nature being what it is, take a look himself in case it was nothing. He would not want his partner to think him jumpy.

Human nature won and the man made his way to the kitchen door. He peered through the glass. Rudy heard a key turn and bolts being withdrawn as the handle was depressed.

The door opened and the man took a step outside, and peered intently at where he thought he had seen the light in the bushes. He tentatively moved forward still concentrating on a point at the bottom of the garden. He would have taken another pace forward if Rudy had not crept silently behind him, palmed his pistol and brought the butt of the Sig Sauer crashing down on his right temple. The man dropped like a stone.

Rudy dragged him back against the wall and laid him next to an old cast iron downpipe. Producing a roll of gaffer tape from his pocket he bound the mans wrists and ankles. He next gagged him with the tape. Finally, he passed the roll of tape behind the pipe and round the wrists a number of times. Satisfied, Rudy cautiously entered through the kitchen door.

Moving silently, he crossed in to the sitting room. Instinctively he knew that by turning to the left and moving towards the front of the house, the door on his left would take him in to the lobby and the foot of the stairs. Rudy stood not moving on the first step. He closed his eyes and visualised the last time he was here. Top of the stairs there were two doors, the one to the left was a guest room with en-suite. The other, a bedroom, overlooking the garden. The door directly in front a family bathroom. Moving along three further doors. Two on the left were bedrooms, one at the far end with an e-suite. The one on the front had been the master bedroom. That was where he had found Beck's black bitch of a wife. She opened the door to go downstairs, only to find him stood there, gun in hand, pointing at her.

She had started to scream, but surprisingly shut up when told to do so. He had wanted her to scream, beg for mercy. She just looked at him and asked what he wanted. When he told her he wanted Beck to suffer when he found her murdered body, she just stared back at him. He pushed her towards the top of the stairs, and then told her to get in to the sitting room.

She stood in the centre of the room defying his instruction to sit down. He moved to within inches of her and ran his hand over body. There was no response from her. It did not matter what he did, she did not flinch, she did not utter a sound. Her lack of any emotion infuriated him. He tried to frighten her by telling her he would rape her, and leave her bloodied body spread-eagled on the floor.

At last he got a response, but not the one he wanted. "Jake will find you and kill you, for the useless piece of shit that you are."

Her defiance and sneering riled him and he shot her once through the heart and again through her left eye.

Rudy composed himself and returned to the task at hand. It had to be the two end bedrooms that Beck and the other copper would occupy. Moving soundlessly he listened carefully at the door on the left. Soft snuffling sounds of a person deep in the arms of Morpheus. He depressed the door handle and opened the door a couple of inches. No movement from inside the room. Pushing the door another few inches, he again stopped and waited, listening for any sign that the person in bed was waking. With no discernible activity, Rudy pulled a cloth and bottle from his tunic. Pouring some liquid on the cloth he quickly entered the room and made for the body in the bed. It began to stir as he was still a pace away. The man began to reach under his pillow. Before he could grab whatever he was after, Rudy had clamped the cloth over his mouth and nose and placed his left knee on the arm that was trying to reach a weapon. The mans left hand tried to wrench Rudy's hand away but after what seemed an eternity his struggles died away as he lost consciousness. Reaching under the pillow, Rudy extracted a Glock automatic pistol. He bound the mans hands and ankles and gagged him.

As he left the room, he took the key and inserted it on the outside of the door locking it.

Chapter 55

Jake stirred and lay in bed. What had disturbed him? He listened. He could hear Tony moving about and then it went silent. He was about to roll over and go back to sleep when he heard the lock click on Tony's door. Beginning to realise something was not right he roused himself and sat on the side of the bed. He turned on the bedside lamp and rubbed his eyes. He was contemplating getting on the floor and extracting the shotgun he had secreted under his bed, when the door burst open and he was looking at the snout of a pistol, and a man dressed in camouflage gear. Suddenly he was wide-awake.

As soon as Rudy saw the light go on and shine under the door, he sprang in to action. Throwing open the door he found Jake sitting naked on the edge of the bed. He straightened his right arm placing the barrel of his Glock a foot from Jakes face.

"Let's go downstairs shall we?" Rudy indicated by waving the barrel of his pistol that Jake should move. Jake began to reach for a robe hanging on the back of the door. "Forget that, you won't need it."

"Why should I bother to move? If you're going to kill, me you may as well do it here."

"Tough as your little wife are you? That bitch was begging for mercy by the time I had finished with her. If you don't want me to kill you piece by piece then I would suggest you do as you're told and get down those stairs. Don't worry your little friends in blue won't see you, they are well taken care of."

Jakes mind had cleared a little more since the initial shock and he realised that Aken wanted more than just to shoot him. He needed to torment him and gloat. Jake began to comprehend that this may give him a chance to turn Aken's crowing to his advantage. He began to rise, and took the robe from its hanger and put it on. There was no reaction from Aken.

As they entered the sitting room Rudy told Jake to sit in the armchair that overlooked the garden. Rudy reached in to his tunic extracting a pack of cigarettes and a lighter. "Mind if I smoke?"

"We don't smoke in this house, but go ahead, why should I refuse a condemned man his last request."

Rudy laughed out loud. "Absolutely right if I was the man on death row, but I'm not. Maybe I should ask what your last request is. How would you like me to tell you about your wife and the fun we had before I shot her? God she was good. You must have kept her on short rations, she was gagging for it."

Rudy was disappointed that this evoked no response from Jake. During the lull in Rudy's story telling, Jake smiled at him. Rudy looked annoyed at this. "I should have filmed it for you."

Jake continued to smile. "Your right, she was that good in bed. Difference is she gave herself to me but you would have had to use force, and I know you didn't. You seem to forget I have seen the autopsy report, and she was not abused. The police and I put it down to you being gay. The inspector in charge thought you were probably turned during your first prison spell as a young man, and made the mistake of bending over in the shower to pick up your soap. Is that it Aken, you only like men."

Placing his gun in his left hand, Rudy moved in front of Jake. He dropped his cigarette on the carpet and stubbed it out under his boot. He then swung his fist and caught Jake on the side of his face. Because Jake was that much lower than Rudy, the punch was not that powerful. It still shook Jake, but not as much as he feigned the effect of the blow.

There was a noise from outside the kitchen and Rudy quickly rushed to the back to see what had caused it. Seeing nothing through the glass he opened the door and stepped outside. With nothing out there to account for the disturbance he checked that Cliff was still secured to the drainpipe.

There was nothing amiss so he re-entered the kitchen leaving the door open. Leaning against the sitting room doorframe, he looked at Jake. "Sorry old man but I will have to hurry things along. Wouldn't want to get caught here and I have a plane to catch. Nice private little job out of Blackbushe at first light. Pity really 'cos I wanted to have a nice cosy little chat and maybe see just how tough you really are."

"You sure we can't talk just a while longer. I've really enjoyed your company and don't want you to go, not just yet anyway."

Rudy began to raise his pistol, "Sorry arsehole, but it's time for you to leave the party." As he spoke, there was the clink of glass on glass. Rudy turned to see a wine bottle descending towards his skull He fired and caught his assailant in the lower chest. But couldn't avoid the bottle crashing on to his head.

Jake leapt out of the chair and closed on Rudy as he turned and swung his arm holding the gun back towards Jake. Jake raised his left arm. As Rudy's arm thumped in to his side, he lowered his arm, trapping Rudy's arm. At the same time his right fist swung up and caught Rudy on his left temple. As Rudy tried to clear his head Jake took his head back then with all the force he could muster he brought his forehead crashing on to the bridge of his nose.

The sheer force of it caused the bone to splinter and the cartilage to rupture. Blood and gore splattered all over Jake's face. Jake was amazed Rudy was still standing, although he was hardly in control of his senses.

He reached and grabbed Rudy's gun hand. He closed his hand over Rudy's and moved it between them both, with the barrel turned towards Rudy's lower abdomen. Rudy's finger was still in the trigger guard with Jakes large fist enclosing it.

Putting his mouth close to Rudy's ear he whispered. "Your right Aken, one of us is leaving the party and it's not me." Aken for once in his life had a frightened look on his face. "Well not all of you, but you will be short of balls from now on."

"No! No! Please don't." Rudy said no more but screamed as Jake tightened his hold on Rudy's trigger finger and forced it back. The explosion was thunderous." Jake then positioned the gun lower and caused Rudy to fire another shot in to his leg. Rudy passed out and Jake lowered him to the floor.

Jake went to check his saviour, the man in the kitchen. Picking up the cordless telephone he dialled 999. He was surprised to find there was no blood and the man conscious. After explaining he needed police and an ambulance he gave the man his attention, kneeling down beside him "Who are you? I owe you my life. Do you need an ambulance?"

"No I am wearing a vest. Thank God, he didn't shoot me in the head, aye! I hit my head on the floor when I went down. I'm okay but you need to go outside and see to one of your mates. He's tied to the drainpipe."

Before he could move, there was a shout from outside that the house was surrounded and that whoever was in there should throw their weapon out and come out with their hands raised.

The man on the floor spoke. "Do it before some trigger happy cop shoots you. By the way I'm Karel Leander, we will talk later."

Jake stepped outside with his hands raised and then lay on the decking as instructed.

Chapter 56

Following a few hours spent in the A and E department at The Royal Berkshire Hospital, Jake was taken to the Police Station where he was met by DCI Potter. Tony Bishop and Cliff Morgan were still at the hospital and would stay there overnight. Karel Leander was in the station and Jake would get to meet him later. Meanwhile because Rudy Aken was undergoing three operations caused by gunshot wounds, or having been struck with a heavy object, Potter needed to get a written statement. The DCI explained that although the injuries were serious, they were not life threatening.

Jake explained that although he was groggy from a blow to the side of the head, he had leapt at the chance to at least have a go at saving his own skin after Aken had turned and shot Karel Leander. Aken tried to turn the gun on him but he had got his hand on the barrel to keep it pointing away. Aken had pulled the trigger, only to shoot himself. Jake did not know where Rudy had been shot. He then fired again and all Rudy could think was that he must have hit the floor because he felt no injury. He then head butted Aken who collapsed. Everything was written down and Jake signed the statement.

"Right." Said the DCI. "Now that's out of the way I'll tell you what I know."

"Shit!" thought Jake, "Karel Leander must have seen and heard what happened and given a different statement."

The DCI continued. "Before he went down, Aken is claiming you shot him twice, delighting in the fact you were blowing his bollocks off. As it is the docs think they can save one, but his femur is shattered and although they may be able to repair it, he will always walk with a limp. Mind you where he's going, he'll never be going for walking holidays again. The gun has gone to forensics for examination, so we will soon find out who had their finger on the trigger."

Inwardly Jake smiled.

There was a tap on the door and Karel Leander and Katrijn Spronk came in to the room.

"Mister Beck let me introduce you to a man that we have all been searching for, Joop Van Ess." DCI Potter made the introductions. "Karel is a Dutch undercover cop."

While the newcomers spoke with Jake, the DCI walked in to the office called out to Zoe. Andy Jones looked at Zoe and said, "He'll want some coffees, bet you don't get the tight old bugger to cough up." The others in the room laughed.

Zoe got up and strode over to the DCI. Just loud enough for the others to hear she asked, "Sir are you circumcised?" The room erupted in to raucous laughter. The DCI could not see what was so funny as Zoe turned away and said, "Okay four coffees it is."

A few days later Jake was back in The Pond House for the usual Friday night get together. The atmosphere was altogether more joyous than previous occasions and Jake had explained to Jason although he had not killed the bastard that murdered his wife, he had gone one better and left him crippled for the rest of his life.